9-7-23

D0910877

They were two desperate scavengers in a no-man's land
of radiation and death.

DOOMSDAY CLASSICS

THE
NIGHT
OF THE
LONG KNIVES

Fritz Leiber

DOVER PUBLICATIONS, INC.
MINEOLA, NEW YORK

Copyright

Artwork Copyright © 1960 by Virgil Finlay
All rights reserved.

Bibliographial Note

This Dover edition, first published in 2015, is an unabridged republication of *The Night of the Long Knives*, which was originally published in the January 1960 issue of *Amazing Science Fiction Stories*. The frontispiece illustration by Virgil Finlay is used courtesy of Lail Finlay.

Library of Congress Cataloging-in-Publication Data

Leiber, Fritz, 1910-1992
The night of the long knives / Fritz Leiber. — Dover edition.
    pages ; cm
"This Dover edition, first published in 2015, is an unabridged republication of The Night of the Long Knives, which was originally published in the January 1960 issue of Amazing Science Fiction Stories."
    ISBN 978-0-486-79801-1 — ISBN 0-486-79801-1
    I. Title.
PS3523.E4583N54 2015
813'.54—dc23

2015001136

Manufactured in the United States by Courier Corporation
79801101   2015
www.doverpublications.com

CHAPTER I

Any man who saw you, or even heard your footsteps must be ambushed, stalked and killed, whether needed for food or not. Otherwise, so long as his strength held out, he would be on your trail.

—The Twenty-Fifth Hour,
by Herbert Best

I was one hundred miles from Nowhere—and I mean that literally—when I spotted this girl out of the corner of my eye. I'd been keeping an extra lookout because I still expected the other undead bugger left over from the murder party at Nowhere to be stalking me.

I'd been following a line of high voltage towers all canted over at the same gentlemanly tipsy angle by an old blast from the Last War. I judged the girl was going in the same general direction and was being edged over toward my course by a drift of dust that even at my distance showed dangerous metallic gleams and dark humps that might be dead men or cattle.

She looked slim, dark topped, and on guard. Small like me and like me wearing a scarf loosely around the lower half of her face in the style of the old buckaroos.

We didn't wave or turn our heads or give the slightest indication we'd seen each other as our paths slowly converged. But we were intensely, minutely watchful—I knew I was and she had better be.

Overhead the sky was a low dust haze, as always. I don't remember what a high sky looks like. Three years ago I think I saw Venus. Or it may have been Sirius or Jupiter.

The hot smoky light was turning from the amber of midday to the bloody bronze of evening.

The line of towers I was following showed the faintest spread in the direction of their canting—they must have been only a few miles from blast center. As I passed each one I could see where the metal on the blast side had been eroded—vaporized by the original blast, mostly smoothly, but with welts and pustules where the metal had merely melted and run. I supposed the lines the towers carried had all been vaporized too, but with the haze I couldn't be sure, though I did see three dark blobs up there that might be vultures perching.

From the drift around the foot of the nearest tower a human skull peered whitely. That is rather unusual. Years later now you still see more dead bodies with the meat on them than skeletons. Intense radiation has killed their bacteria and preserved them indefinitely from decay, just like the packaged meat in the last advertisements. In fact such bodies are one of the signs of a really hot drift—you avoid them. The vultures pass up such poisonously hot carrion too— they've learned their lesson.

Ahead some big gas tanks began to loom up, like deformed battle-ships and flat-tops in a smoke screen, their prows being the juncture of the natural curve of the off-blast side with the massive concavity of the on-blast side.

None of the three other buggers and me had had too clear an idea of where Nowhere had been—hence, in part, the name—but I knew in a general way that I was somewhere in the Deathlands between Porter County and Ouachita Parish, probably much nearer the former.

It's a real mixed-up America we've got these days, you know, with just the faintest trickle of a sense of identity left, like a guy in the paddedest cell in the most locked up ward in the whole loony bin. If a time traveler from mid Twentieth Century hopped forward to it across the few intervening years and looked at a map of it, if any-body has a map of it, he'd think that the map had run—that it had got some sort of disease that had swollen a few tiny parts beyond all bounds, paper tumors, while most of the other parts, the parts he remembered carrying names in such big print and showing such bold colors, had shrunk to nothingness.

To the east he'd see Atlantic Highlands and Savannah Fortress. To the west, Walla Walla Territory, Pacific Palisades, and Los Alamos—and there he'd see an actual change in the coastline, I'm told, where three of the biggest stockpiles of fusionables let go and opened Death Valley to the sea—so that Los Alamos is closer to being a port. Centrally he'd find Porter County and Manteno Asylum surprisingly close together near the Great Lakes, which are tilted and spilled out a bit toward the southwest with the big quake. South-centrally: Ouachita Parish inching up the Mississippi from old Louisiana under the cruel urging of the Fisher Sheriffs.

Those he'd find and a few, a very few other places, including a couple I suppose I haven't heard of. Practically all of them would surprise him—no one can predict what scraps of a blasted nation are going to hang onto a shred of organization and ruthlessly maintain it and very slowly and very jealously extend it.

But biggest of all, occupying practically all the map, reducing all those swollen localities I've mentioned back to tiny blobs, bounding most of America and thrusting its jetty pseudopods everywhere, he'd see the great inkblot of the Deathlands. I don't know how else than by an area of solid, absolutely unrelieved black you'd represent the Deathlands with its multicolored radioactive dusts and its skimpy freightage of lonely Deathlanders, each bound on his murderous, utterly pointless, but utterly absorbing business—an area where names like Nowhere, It, Anywhere, and the Place are the most natural thing in the world when a few of us decide to try to pad down together for a few nervous months or weeks.

As I say, I was somewhere in the Deathlands near Manteno Asylum.

The girl and me were getting closer now, well within pistol or dart range though beyond any but the most expert or lucky knife throw.

She wore boots and a weathered long-sleeved shirt and jeans. The black topping was hair, piled high in an elaborate coiffure that was held in place by twisted shavings of bright metal. A fine bug-trap, I told myself.

In her left hand, which was closest to me, she carried a dart gun, pointed away from me, across her body. It was the kind of potent tiny crossbow you can't easily tell whether the spring is loaded. Back around on her left hip a small leather satchel was strapped to her belt. Also on the same side were two sheathed knives, one of which was an oddity—it had no handle, just the bare tang. For nothing but throwing, I guessed.

I let my own left hand drift a little closer to my Banker's Special in its open holster—Ray Baker's great psychological weapon, though (who knows?) the two .38 cartridges it contained might actually fire. The one I'd put to the test at Nowhere had, and very lucky for me.

She seemed to be hiding her right arm from me. Then I spotted the weapon it held, one you don't often see, a stevedore's hook. She *was* hiding her right hand, all right, she had the long sleeve pulled down over it so just the hook stuck out. I asked myself if the hand were perhaps covered with radiation scars or sores or otherwise disfigured. We Deathlanders have our vanities. I'm sensitive about my baldness.

Then she let her right arm swing more freely and I saw how short it was. She had no right hand. The hook was attached to the wrist stump.

I judged she was about ten years younger than me. I'm pushing forty, I think, though some people have judged I'm younger. No way of my knowing for sure. In this life you forget trifles like chronology.

Anyway, the age difference meant she would have quicker reflexes. I'd have to keep that in mind.

The greenishly glinting dust drift that I'd judged she was avoiding swung closer ahead. The girl's left elbow gave a little kick to the satchel on her hip and there was a sudden burst of irregular ticks that almost made me start. I steadied myself and concentrated on thinking whether I should attach any special significance to her carrying a Geiger counter. Naturally it wasn't the sort of thinking that interfered in any way with my watchfulness—you quickly lose the habit of that kind of thinking in the Deathlands or you lose something else.

It could mean she was some sort of greenhorn. Most of us old-timers can visually judge the heat of a dust drift or crater or rayed area more reliably than any instrument. Some buggers claim they just feel it, though I've never known any of the latter too eager to navigate in unfamiliar country at night—which you'd think they'd be willing to do if they could feel heat blind.

But she didn't look one bit like a tenderfoot—like for instance some citizeness newly banished from Manteno. Or like some Porter burgher's unfaithful wife or troublesome girlfriend whom he'd personally carted out beyond the ridges of cleaned-out hot dust that help guard such places, and then abandoned in revenge or from boredom—and they call themselves civilized, those cultural queers!

No, she looked like she *belonged* in the Deathlands. But then why the counter?

Her eyes might be bad, real bad. I didn't think so. She raised her boot an extra inch to step over a little jagged fragment of concrete. No.

Maybe she was just a born double-checker, using science to back up knowledge based on experience as rich as my own or richer. I've met the super-careful type before. They mostly get along pretty well, but they tend to be a shade too slow in the clutches.

Maybe she was *testing* the counter, planning to use it some other way or trade it for something.

Maybe she made a practice of traveling by night! Then the counter made good sense. But then why use it by day? Why reveal it to me in any case?

Was she trying to convince me that she was a greenhorn? Or had she hoped that the sudden noise would throw me off guard? But who would go to the trouble of carrying a Geiger counter for such devious purposes? And wouldn't she have waited until we got closer before trying the noise gambit?

Think-shmink—it gets you nowhere!

She kicked off the counter with another bump of her elbow and started to edge in toward me faster. I turned the thinking all off and gave my whole mind to watchfulness.

Soon we were barely more than eight feet apart, almost within lunging range without even the preliminary one-two step, and still we hadn't spoken or looked straight at each other, though being that close we'd had to cant our heads around a bit to keep each other in peripheral vision. Our eyes would be on each other steadily for five or six seconds, then dart forward an instant to check for rocks and holes in the trail we were following in parallel. A cultural queer from one of the "civilized" places would have found it funny, I suppose, if he'd been able to watch us perform in an arena or from behind armor glass for his exclusive pleasure.

The girl had eyebrows as black as her hair, which in its piled-up and metal-knotted savagery called to mind African queens despite her typical pale complexion—very little ultraviolet gets through the dust. From the inside corner of her right eye socket a narrow radiation scar ran up between her eyebrows and across her forehead at a rakish angle until it disappeared under a sweep of hair at the upper left corner of her forehead.

I'd been smelling her, of course, for some time.

I could even tell the color of her eyes now. They were blue. It's a color you never see. Almost no dusts have a bluish cast, there are few blue objects except certain dark steels, the sky never gets very far away from the orange range, though it is green from time to time, and water reflects the sky.

Yes, she had blue eyes, blue eyes and that jaunty scar, blue eyes and that jaunty scar and a dart gun and a steel hook for a right hand, and we were walking side by side, eight feet apart, not an inch closer, still not looking straight at each other, still not saying a word, and I realized that the initial period of unadulterated watchfulness was over, that I'd had adequate opportunity to inspect this girl and size her up, and that night was coming on fast, and that here I was, once again, back with *the problem of the two urges.*

I could try either to kill her or go to bed with her.

I know that at this point the cultural queers (and certainly our imaginary time traveler from mid Twentieth Century) would make a great noise about not understanding and not believing in the genuineness of the simple urge to murder that governs the lives of us Deathlanders. Like detective-story pundits, they would say that a man or woman murders for gain, or concealment of crime, or from thwarted sexual desire or outraged sexual possessiveness—and maybe they would list a few other "rational" motives—but not, they would say, just for the simple sake of murder, for the sure release and relief it gives, for the sake of wiping out one recognizable bit more (the closest bit we can, since those of us with the courage or lazy rationality to wipe out ourselves have long since done so)—wiping out one recognizable bit more of the whole miserable, unutterably disgusting human mess. Unless, they would say, a person is completely insane, which is actually how all outsiders view us Deathlanders. They can think of us in no other way.

I guess cultural queers and time travelers simply *don't* understand, though to be so blind it seems to me that they have to overlook much of the history of the Last War and of the subsequent years, especially the mushrooming of crackpot cults with a murder tinge: the werewolf gangs, the Berserkers and Amuckers, the revival of Shiva worship and the Black Mass, the machine wreckers, the kill-the-killers movements, the new witchcraft, the Unholy Creepers, the Unconsciousers, the radioactive blue gods and rocket devils of the Atomites, and a dozen other groupings clearly prefiguring Deathlander psychology. Those cults had all been as unpredictable as Thugee or the Dancing Madness of the Middle Ages or the Children's Crusade, yet they had happened just the same.

But cultural queers are good at overlooking things. They have to be, I suppose. They think they're humanity growing again. Yes, despite their laughable warpedness and hysterical crippledness, they actually believe—each howlingly different community of them—that they're the new Adams and Eves. They're all excited about themselves and whether or not they wear fig leaves. They don't carry with them, twenty-four hours a day, like us Deathlanders do, the burden of all that was forever lost.

Since I've gone this far I'll go a bit further and make the paradoxical admission that even us Deathlanders don't really understand our urge to murder. Oh, we have our rationalizations of it, just like everyone has of his ruling passion—we call ourselves junkmen, scavengers, gangrene surgeons; we sometimes believe we're doing the person we kill the ultimate kindness, yes and get slobbery tearful about it afterwards; we sometimes tell ourselves we've finally found and are rubbing out the one man or woman who was responsible for everything; we talk, mostly to ourselves, about the aesthetics of homicide; we occasionally admit, but only each to himself alone, that we're just plain nuts.

But we don't really understand our urge to murder, we only *feel* it.

At the hateful sight of another human being, we feel it begins to grow in us until it becomes an overpowering impulse that jerks us, like a puppet is jerked by its strings, into the act itself or its attempted commission.

Like I was feeling it grow in me now as we did this parallel death-march through the reddening haze, me and this girl and our problem. This girl with the blue eyes and the jaunty scar.

The problem of the *two* urges, I said. The other urge, the sexual, is one that I know all cultural queers (and certainly our time traveler) would claim to know all about. Maybe they do. But I wonder if they understand how intense it can be with us Deathlanders when it's the only release (except maybe liquor and drugs, which we seldom can get and even more rarely dare use)—the only complete release, even though a brief one, from the overpowering loneliness and from the tyranny of the urge to kill.

To embrace, to possess, to glut lust on, yes even briefly to love, briefly to shelter in—that was good, that was a relief and release to be treasured.

But it couldn't last. You could draw it out, prop it up perhaps for a few days, for a month even (though sometimes not for a single night)—you might even start to talk to each other a little, after a while—but it could never last. The glands always tire, if nothing else.

Murder was the only *final* solution, the only *permanent* release. Only us Deathlanders know how good it feels. But then after the kill the loneliness would come back, redoubled, and after a while I'd meet another hateful human . . .

Our problem of the two urges. As I watched this girl slogging along parallel to me, as I kept constant watch on her of course, I wondered how *she* was feeling the two urges. Was she attracted to the ridgy scars on my cheeks half revealed by my scarf?—to me they have a pleasing symmetry. Was she wondering how my head and face looked without the black felt skullcap low-visored over my eyes? Or was she thinking mostly of that hook swinging into my throat under the chin and dragging me down ?

I couldn't tell. She looked as poker-faced as I was trying to.

For that matter, I asked myself, how was *I* feeling the two urges?—how was I feeling them as I watched this girl with the blue eyes and the jaunty scar and the arrogantly thinned lips that asked to be smashed, and the slender throat?—and I realized that there was no way to describe that, not even to myself. I could only feel the two urges grow in me, side by side, like monstrous twins, until they would simply be too big for my taut body and one of them would have to get out fast.

I don't know which one of us started to slow down first, it happened so gradually, but the dust puffs that rise from the ground of the Deathlands under even the lightest treading became smaller and smaller around our steps and finally vanished altogether, and we were standing still. Only then did I notice the obvious physical trigger for our stopping. An old freeway ran at right angles across our path. The shoulder by which we'd approached it was sharply eroded, so that the pavement, which even had a shallow cave eroded under it, was a good three feet above the level of our path, forming a low wall. From where I'd stopped I could almost reach out and touch the rough-edged smooth-topped concrete. So could she.

We were right in the midst of the gas tanks now, six or seven of them towered around us, squeezed like beer cans by the decade-old blast but their metal looking sound enough until you became aware of the red light showing through in odd patterns of dots and dashes where vaporization or later erosion had been complete. Almost but not quite lace-work. Just ahead of us, right across the freeway, was the six-storey skeletal structure of an old cracking plant, sagged like the power towers away from the blast and the lower storeys drifted with piles and ridges and smooth gobbets of dust.

The light was getting redder and smokier every minute.

With the cessation of the physical movement of walking, which is always some sort of release for emotions, I could feel the twin urges growing faster in me. But that was all right, I told myself—this was the crisis, as she must realize too, and that should key us up to bear the urges a little longer without explosion.

I was the first to start to turn my head. For the first time I looked straight into her eyes and she into mine. And as always happens at such times, a third urge appeared abruptly, an urge momentarily as strong as the other two—the urge to speak, to tell and ask all about it. But even as I started to phrase the first crazily happy greeting, my throat lumped, as I'd known it would, with the awful melancholy of all that was forever lost, with the uselessness of any communication, with the impossibility of recreating the past, our individual pasts, any pasts. And as it always does, the third urge died.

I could tell she was feeling that ultimate pain just like me. I could see her eyelids squeeze down on her eyes and her face lift and her shoulders go back as she swallowed hard.

She was the first to start to lay aside a weapon. She took two side-wise steps toward the freeway and reached her whole left arm further across her body and laid the dart gun on the concrete and drew back her hand from it about six inches. At the same time looking at me hard—fiercely angrily, you'd say—across her left shoulder. She had the experienced duelist's trick of seeming to look into my eyes but actually focussing on my mouth. I was using the same gimmick myself—it's tiring to look straight into another person's eyes and it can put you off guard.

My left side was nearest the wall so I didn't for the moment have the problem of reaching across my body. I took the same sidewise steps she had and using just two fingers, very gingerly—*disarmingly*, I hoped—I lifted my antique firearm from its holster and laid it on the concrete and drew back my hand from it all the way. Now it was up to her again, or should be. Her hook was going to be quite a problem, I realized, but we needn't come to it right away.

She temporized by successively unsheathing the two knives at her left side and laying them beside the dart gun. Then she stopped and her look told me plainly that it was up to me.

Now I am a bugger who believes in carrying *one perfect knife*—otherwise, I know for a fact, you'll go knife-happy and end up by weighing yourself down with dozens, literally. So I am naturally very reluctant to get out of touch in any way with Mother, who is a little rusty along the sides but made of the toughest and most sharpenable alloy steel I've ever run across.

Still, I was most curious to find out what she'd do about that hook, so I finally laid Mother on the concrete beside the .38 and rested my hands lightly on my hips, all ready to enjoy myself—at least I hoped I gave that impression.

She smiled, it was almost a nice smile—by now we'd let our scarves drop since we weren't raising any more dust—and then she took hold of the hook with her left hand and started to unscrew it from the leather-and-metal base fitting over her stump.

Of course, I told myself. And her second knife, the one without a grip, must be that way so she could screw its tang into the base when she wanted a knife on her right hand instead of a hook. I ought to have guessed.

I grinned my admiration of her mechanical ingenuity and immediately unhitched my knapsack and laid it beside my weapons. Then a thought occurred to me. I opened the knapsack and moving my hand slowly and very openly so she'd have no reason to suspect a ruse, I drew out a blanket and, trying to show her both sides of it in the process, as if I were performing some damned conjuring trick, dropped it gently on the ground between us.

She unsnapped the straps on her satchel that fastened it to her belt and laid it aside and then she took off her belt too, slowly drawing it through the wide loops of weathered denim. Then she looked meaningfully at my belt.

I had to agree with her. Belts, especially heavy-buckled ones like ours, can be nasty weapons. I removed mine. Simultaneously each belt joined its corresponding pile of weapons and other belongings.

She shook her head, not in any sort of negation, and ran her fingers into the black hair at several points, to show me it hid no weapon, then looked at me questioningly. I nodded that I was satisfied—I hadn't seen anything run out of it, by the way. Then she looked up at my black skullcap and she raised her eyebrows and smiled again, this time with a spice of mocking anticipation.

In some ways I hate to part with that headpiece more than I do with Mother. Not really because of its sandwiched lead-mesh inner lining—if the rays haven't baked my brain yet they never will and I'm sure that the patches of lead mesh sewed into my pants over my loins give a lot more practical protection. But I was getting real attracted to this girl by now and there are times when a person must make a sacrifice of his vanity. I whipped off my stylish black felt and tossed it on my pile and dared her to laugh at my shiny egg top.

Strangely she didn't even smile. She parted her lips and ran her tongue along the upper one. I gave an eager grin in reply, an incautiously wide one, and she saw my plates flash.

My plates are something rather special though they are by no means unique. Back toward the end of the Last War, when it was obvious to any realist how bad things were going to be, though not how strangely terrible, a number of people, like myself, had all their teeth jerked and replaced with durable plates. I went some of them one better. My plates were stainless steel biting and chewing ridges, smooth continuous ones that didn't attempt to copy individual teeth. A person who looks closely at a slab of chewing tobacco, say, I offer him will be puzzled by the smoothly curved incision, made as if by a razor blade mounted on the arm of a compass. Magnetic powder buried in my gums makes for a real nice fit.

This sacrifice was worse than my hat and Mother combined, but I could see the girl expected me to make it and would take no substitutes, and in this attitude I had to admit that she showed very sound judgment, because I keep the incisor parts of those plates filed to razor sharpness. I have to be careful about my tongue and lips but I figure it's worth it. With my dental scimitars I can in a wink bite out a chunk of throat and windpipe or jugular, though I've never had occasion to do so yet.

For the first minute it made me feel like an old man, a real dodderer, but by now the attraction this girl had for me was getting irrational. I carefully laid the two plates on top of my knapsack.

In return, as a sort of reward you might say, she opened her mouth wide and showed me what was left of her own teeth—about two-thirds of them, a patchwork of tartar and gold.

We took off our boots, pants and shirts, she watching very suspiciously—I knew she'd been skeptical of my carrying only one knife.

Oddly perhaps, considering how touchy I am about my baldness, I felt no sensitivity about revealing the lack of hair on my chest and in fact a sort of pride in displaying the slanting radiation scars that have replaced it, though they are crawling keloids of the ugliest, bumpiest sort. I guess to me such scars are tribal insignia—one-man and one-woman tribes of course. No question but that the scar on the girl's forehead had been the first focus of my desire for her and it still added to my interest.

By now we weren't staying as perfectly on guard or watching each other's clothing for concealed weapons as carefully as we should—I know I wasn't. It was getting dark fast, there wasn't much time left, and the other interest was simply becoming too great.

We were still automatically careful about how we did things. For instance the way we took off our pants was like ballet, simultaneously crouching a little on the left foot and whipping the right leg out of its sheath in one movement, all ready to jump without tripping ourselves if the other person did anything funny, and then skinning down the left pants-leg with a movement almost as swift.

But as I say it was getting too late for perfect watchfulness, in fact for any kind of effective watchfulness at all. The complexion of the whole situation was changing in a rush. The possibilities of dealing or receiving death—along with the chance of the minor indignity of cannibalism, which some of us practice—were suddenly gone, all gone. It was going to be all right this time, I was telling myself. This was the time it would be different, this was the time love would last, this was the time lust would be the firm foundation for understanding and trust, this time there would be really safe sleeping. This girl's body would be home for me, a beautiful tender inexhaustibly exciting home, and mine for her, for always.

As she threw off her shirt, the last darkly red light showed me another smooth slantwise scar, this one around her hips, like a narrow girdle that has slipped down a little on one side.

CHAPTER II

Murder most foul, as in the best it is;
But this most foul, strange and unnatural.

—Hamlet

WHEN I woke the light was almost full amber and I could feel no flesh against mine, only the blanket under me. I very slowly rolled over and there she was, sitting on the corner of the blanket not two feet from me, combing her long black hair with a big, wide-toothed comb she'd screwed into the leather-and-metal cap over her wrist stump.

She'd put on her pants and shirt, but the former were rolled up to her knees and the latter, though tucked in, wasn't buttoned.

She was looking at me, contemplating me you might say, quite dreamily but with a faint, easy smile.

I smiled back at her.

It was lovely.

Too lovely. There had to be something wrong with it.

There was. Oh, nothing big. Just a solitary trifle—nothing worth noticing really.

But the tiniest solitary things can sometimes be the most irritating, like *one* mosquito.

When I'd first rolled over she'd been combing her hair straight back, revealing a wedge of baldness following the continuation of her forehead scar deep back across her scalp. Now with a movement that was swift though not hurried-looking she swept the mass of her

15

hair forward and to the left, so that it covered the bald area. Also her lips straightened out.

I was hurt. She shouldn't have hidden her bit of baldness, it was something we had in common, something that brought us closer. And she shouldn't have stopped smiling at just that moment. Didn't she realize I loved that blaze on her scalp just as much as any other part of her, that she no longer had any need to practice vanity in front of me?

Didn't she realize that as soon as she stopped smiling, her contemplative stare became an insult to me? What right had she to stare, critically I felt sure, at my bald head? What right had she to know about the nearly-healed ulcer on my left shin?—that was a piece of information worth a man's life in a fight. What right had she to cover up, anyways, while I was still naked? She ought to have waked me up so that we could have got dressed as we'd undressed, together. There were lots of things wrong with her manners.

Oh, I know that if I'd been able to think calmly, maybe if I'd just had some breakfast or a little coffee inside me, or even if there'd been some hot breakfast to eat at that moment, I'd have recognized my irritation for the irrational, one-mosquito surge of negative feeling that it was.

Even without breakfast, if I'd just had the knowledge that there was a reasonably secure day ahead of me in which there'd be an opportunity for me to straighten out my feelings, I wouldn't have been irked, or at least being irked wouldn't have bothered me terribly.

But a sense of security is an even rarer commodity in the Deathlands than a hot breakfast.

Given just the ghost of a sense of security and/or some hot breakfast, I'd have told myself that she was merely being amusingly coquettish about her bald streak and her hair, that it was natural for a woman to try to preserve some mystery about herself in front of the man she beds with.

But you get leery of any kind of mystery in the Deathlands. It makes you frightened and angry, like it does an animal. Mystery is for cultural queers, strictly. The only way for two people to get along together in the Deathlands, even for a while, is never to hide anything and never to make a move that doesn't have an immediate clear explanation. You can't talk, you see, certainly not at first, and so you can't explain anything (most explanations are just lies and dreams, anyway), so you have to be doubly careful and explicit about everything you do.

This girl wasn't being either. Right now, on top of her other gaucheries, she was unscrewing the comb from her wrist—an unfriendly if not quite a hostile act, as anyone must admit.

Understand, please, I wasn't *showing* any of these negative reactions of mine any more than she was showing hers, except for her stopping smiling. In fact *I hadn't* stopped smiling, I was playing the game to the hilt.

But inside me everything was stewed up and the other urge had come back and presently it would begin to grow again. That's the trouble, you know, with sex as a solution to the problem of the two urges. It's fine while it lasts but it wears itself out and then you're back with Urge Number One and you have nothing left to balance it with.

Oh, I wouldn't kill this girl today, I probably wouldn't seriously think of killing her for a month or more, but Old Urge Number One would be there and growing, mostly under cover, all the time. Of course there were things I could do to slow its growth, lots of little gimmicks, in fact—I was pretty experienced at this business.

For instance, I could take a shot at talking to her pretty soon. For a catchy starter, I could tell her about Nowhere, how these five other buggers and me found ourselves independently skulking along after this scavenging expedition from Porter, how we naturally joined forces in that situation, how we set a pitfall for their alky-powered jeep and wrecked it and them, how when our haul turned out to be unexpectedly big the four of us left from the kill chummied up and padded down together and amused each other for a while and played games, you might say. Why, at one point we even had an old crank phonograph going and read some books. And, of course, how when the loot gave out and the fun wore off, we had our murder party and I survived along with, I think, a bugger named Jerry—at any rate, he was gone when the blood stopped spurting, and I'd had no stomach for tracking him, though I probably should have.

And in return she could tell me how she had killed off her last set of girlfriends, or boyfriends, or friend, or whatever it was.

After that, we could have a go at exchanging news, rumors and speculations about local, national and world events. Was it true that Atlantic Highlands had planes of some sort or were they from Europe? Were they actually crucifying the Deathlanders around Walla Walla or only nailing up their dead bodies as dire warnings to others such? Had Manteno made Christianity compulsory yet, or were they still tolerating Zen Buddhists? Was it true that Los Alamos had been completely wiped out by plague, but the area taboo to Deathlanders because of the robot guards they'd left behind—metal guards eight feet tall who tramped across the white sands, wailing. Did they still have free love in Pacific Palisades? Did she know there'd been a pitched battle fought by expeditionary forces from Ouachita and Savannah Fortress? Over the loot of Birmingham, apparently, after yellow fever had finished off that principality. Had she rooted out any "observers" lately?—some of the "civilized" communities, the more "scientific" ones, try to maintain a few weather stations and the like in the Deathlands, camouflaging them elaborately and manning them with one or two impudent characters to whom we give a hard time if we uncover them. Had she heard the tale that was going around that South America and the French Riviera had survived the Last War absolutely untouched?—and the obviously ridiculous rider that they had blue skies there and saw stars every third night ? Did she think that subsequent conditions were showing that the Earth actually had plunged into an interstellar dust cloud coincidentally with the start of the Last War (the dust cloud used as a cover for the first attacks, some said) or did she still hold with the majority that the dust was solely of atomic origin with a little help from volcanoes and dry spells? How many green sunsets had she seen in the last year?

After we'd chewed over those racy topics and some more like them, and incidentally got bored with guessing and fabricating, we might, if we felt especially daring and conversation were going particularly well, even take a chance on talking a little about our childhoods, about how things were before the Last War (though she was almost too young for that)—about the *little* things we remembered—the big things were much too dangerous topics to venture on and sometimes even the little memories could suddenly twist you up as if you'd swallowed lye.

But after that there wouldn't be anything left to talk about. Anything you'd risk talking about, that is. For instance, no matter how long we talked, it was very unlikely that we'd either of us tell the other anything complete or very accurate about how we lived from day to day, about our techniques of surviving and staying sane or at least functional—that would be too imprudent, it would go too much against the grain of any player of the murder game. Would I tell her, or anyone, about how I worked the ruses of playing dead and disguising myself as a woman, about my trick of picking a path just before dark and then circling back to it by a pre-surveyed route, about the chess games I played with myself, about the bottle of green, terribly hot-looking powder I carried to sprinkle behind me to bluff off pursuers? A fat chance of my revealing things like that!

And when all the talk was over, what would it have gained us? Our minds would be filled with a lot of painful stuff better kept buried—meaningless hopes, scraps of vicarious living in "cultured" communities, memories that were nothing but melancholy given concrete form. The melancholy is easiest to bear when it's the diffused background for everything; and all garbage is best kept in the can. Oh yes, our talking would have gained us a few more days of infatuation, of phantom security, but those we could have—almost as many of them, at any rate—without talking.

For instance things were smoothing over already between her and me again and I no longer felt quite so irked. She'd replaced the comb with an inoffensive-looking pair of light pliers and was doing up her hair with the metal shavings. And I was acting as if content to watch her, as in a way I was. I'd still made no move to get dressed.

She looked real sweet, you know, primping herself that way. Her face was a little flat, but it was young, and the scar gave it just the fillip it needed.

But what was going on behind that forehead right now, I asked myself? I felt real psychic this morning, my mind as clear as a bottle of White Rock you find miraculously unbroken in a blasted tavern, and the answers to the question I'd asked myself came effortlessly.

She was telling herself she'd got herself a man again, a man who was adequate in the primal clutch (I gave myself that pat on the back), and that she wouldn't have to be plagued and have her safety endangered by *that* kind of mind-dulling restlessness and yearning for a while.

She was lightly playing around with ideas about how she'd found a home and a protector, knowing she was kidding herself, that it was the most gimcracky feminine make-believe, but enjoying it just the same.

She was sizing me up, deciding in detail just what I went for in a woman, what whetted my interest, so she could keep that roused as long as seemed desirable or prudent to her to continue our relation.

She was kicking herself, only lightly to begin with, because she hadn't taken any precautions—because we who've escaped hot death against all reasonable expectations by virtue of some incalculable resistance to the ills of radioactivity, quite often find we've escaped sterility too. If she should become pregnant, she was telling herself, then she had a real sticky business ahead of her where no man could be trusted for a second.

And because she was thinking of this and because she was obviously a realistic Deathlander, she was reminding herself that a woman is basically less impulsive and daring and resourceful than a man and so had always better be sure she gets in the first blow. She would be thinking that I was a realist myself and a smart man, one able to understand her predicament quite clearly—and because of that a much sooner danger to her. She was feeling Old Number One Urge starting to grow in her again and wondering whether it mightn't be wisest to give it the hot-house treatment.

That is the trouble with a clear mind. For a little while you see things as they really are and you can accurately predict how they're going to shape the future . . . and then suddenly you realize you've predicted yourself a week or a month into the future and you can't live the intervening time any more because you've already imagined it in detail. People who live in communities, even the cultural queers of our maimed era, aren't much bothered by it—there must be some sort of blinkers they hand you out along with the key to the city—but in the Deathlands it's a fairly common phenomenon and there's no hiding from it.

Me and my clear mind!—once again it had done me out of days of fun, changed a thoroughly-explored love affair into a one night stand. Oh, there was no question about it, this girl and I were finished, right this minute, as of now, because she was just as psychic as I was this morning and had sensed every last thing that I'd been thinking.

With a movement smooth enough not to look rushed I swung into a crouch. She was on her knees faster than that, her left hand hovering over the little set of tools for her stump, which like any good mechanic she'd lined up neatly on the edge of the blanket—the hook, the comb, a long telescoping fork, a couple of other items, and the knife. I'd grabbed a handful of blanket, ready to jerk it from under her. She'd seen that I'd grabbed it. Our gazes dueled.

There was a high-pitched whine over our heads! Quite loud from the start, though it sounded as if it were very deep up in the haze. It swiftly dropped in pitch and volume.

The top of the skeletal cracking plant across the freeway glowed with St. Elmo's fire! Three times it glowed that way, so bright we could see the violet-blue flames of it reaching up despite the full amber daylight.

The whine died away but in the last moment, paradoxically, it seemed to be coming closer!

This shared threat—for any unexpected event is a threat in the Deathlands and a mysterious event doubly so—put a stop to our murder game. The girl and I were buddies again, buddies to be relied on in a pinch, for the duration of the threat at least. No need to say so or to reassure each other of the fact in any way, it was taken for granted. Besides, there was no time. We had to use every second allowed us in getting ready for whatever was coming.

First I grabbed up Mother. Then I relieved myself—fear made it easy. Then I skinned into my pants and boots, slapped in my teeth, thrust the blanket and knapsack into the shallow cave under the edge of the freeway, looking around me all the time so as not to be surprised from any quarter.

Meanwhile the girl had put on her boots, located her dart gun, unscrewed the pliers from her stump, put the knife in, and was arranging her scarf so it made a sling for the maimed arm—I wondered why but had no time to waste guessing, even if I'd wanted to, for at that moment a small dull silver plane, beetle-shaped more than anything else, loomed out of the haze beyond the cracking plant and came silently drifting down toward us.

The girl thrust her satchel into the cave and along with it her dart gun. I caught her idea and tucked Mother into my pants behind my back.

I'd thought from the first glimpse of it that the plane was disabled—I guess it was its silence that gave me the idea. This theory was confirmed when one of its very stubby wings or vanes touched a corner pillar of the cracking plant. The plane was moving in too slow a glide to be wrecked, in fact it was moving in a slower glide than I would have believed possible—but then it's many years since I have seen a plane in flight.

It wasn't wrecked but the little collision spun it around twice in a lazy circle and it landed on the freeway with a scuffing noise not fifty feet from us. You couldn't exactly say it had crashed in, but it stayed at an odd tilt. It looked crippled all right.

An oval door in the plane opened and a man dropped lightly out on the concrete. And what a man! He was nearer seven feet tall than six, close-cropped blond hair, face and hands richly tanned, the rest of him covered by trim garments of a gleaming gray. He must have weighed as much as the two of us together, but he was beautifully built, muscular yet supple-seeming. His face looked brightly intelligent and even-tempered and kind.

Yes, kind!—damn him! It wasn't enough that his body should fairly glow with a health and vitality that was an insult to our seared skins and stringy muscles and ulcers and half-rotted stomachs and half-arrested cancers, he had to look kind too—the sort of man who would put you to bed and take care of you, as if you were some sort of interesting sick fox, and maybe even say a little prayer for you, and all manner of other abominations.

I don't think I could have endured my fury standing still. Fortunately there was no need to. As if we'd rehearsed the whole thing for hours, the girl and I scrambled up onto the freeway and scurried toward the man from the plane, cunningly swinging away from each other so that it would be harder for him to watch the two of us at once, but not enough to make it obvious that we attended an attack from two quarters.

We didn't run though we covered the ground as fast as we dared— running would have been too much of a give-away too, and the Pilot, which was how I named him to myself, had a strange-looking small gun in his right hand. In fact the way we moved was part of our act—I dragged one leg as if it were crippled and the girl faked another sort of limp, one that made her approach a series of half curtsies. Her arm in the sling was all twisted, but at the same time she was accidently showing her breasts—I remember *thinking you won't distract this breed bull that way, sister, he probably has a harem of six-foot heifers.* I had my head thrown back and my hands stretched out supplicatingly. Meanwhile the both of us were babbling a blue streak. I was rapidly croaking something like, "Mister for God's sake save my pal he's hurt a lot worse'n I am not a hundred yards away he's dyin' mister he's dyin' o' thirst his tongue's black'n all swole up oh save him mister save my pal he's not a hundred yards away he's dyin' mister dyin'—" and she was singsonging an even worse rigamarole about how "they" were after us from Porter and going to crucify us because we believed in science and how they'd already impaled her mother and her ten-year-old sister and a lot more of the same.

It didn't matter that our stories didn't fit or make sense, the babble had a convincing tone and getting us closer to this guy, which was all that counted. He pointed his gun at me and then I could see him hesitate and I thought exultingly *it's a lot of healthy meat you got there, mister, but it's tame meat, mister, tame!*

He compromised by taking a step back and sort of hooting at us and waving us off with his left hand, as if we were a couple of stray dogs.

It was greatly to our advantage that we'd acted without hesitation, and I don't think we'd have been able to do that except that we'd been all set to kill each other when he dropped in. Our muscles and nerves and minds were keyed for instant ruthless attack. And some "civilized" people still say the the urge to murder doesn't contribute to self-preservation!

We were almost close enough now and he was steeling himself to shoot and I remember wondering for a split second what his damn gun did to you, and then me and the girl had started the alternation routine. I'd stop dead, as if completely cowed by the threat of his weapon, and as he took note of it she'd go in a little further, and as his gaze shifted to her she'd stop dead and I'd go in another foot and then try to make my halt even more convincing as his gaze darted back to me. We worked it perfectly, our rhythm was beautiful, as if we were old dancing partners, though the whole thing was absolutely impromptu.

Still, I honestly don't think we'd ever have got to him if it hadn't been for the distraction that came just then to help us. I could tell, you see, that he'd finally steeled himself and we still weren't quite close enough. He wasn't as tame as I'd hoped. I reached behind me for Mother, determined to do a last-minute rush and leap anyway, when there came this sick scream.

I don't know how else to describe it briefly. It was a scream, feminine for choice, it came from some distance and the direction of the old cracking plant, it had a note of anguish and warning, yet at the same time it was weak and almost faltering you might say and squeaky at the end, as if it came from a person half dead and a throat choked with phlegm. It had all those qualities or a wonderful mimicking of them.

And it had quite an effect on our boy in gray for in the act of shooting me down he started to turn and look over his shoulder.

Oh, it didn't altogether stop him from shooting me. He got me partly covered again as I was in the middle of my lunge. I found out what his gun did to you. My right arm, which was the part he'd covered, just went dead and I finished my lunge slamming up against his iron knees, like a highschool kid trying to block out a pro footballer, with the knife slipping uselessly away from my fingers.

But in the blessed meanwhile the girl had lunged too, not with a slow slash, thank God, but with a high, slicing thrust aimed arrow-straight for a point just under his ear.

She connected and a fan of blood sprayed her full in the face.

I grabbed my knife with my left hand as it fell, scrambled to my feet, and drove the knife at his throat in a round-house swing that happened to come handiest at the time. The point went through his flesh like nothing and jarred against his spine with a violence that I hoped would shock into nervous insensibility the stoutest medulla oblongata and prevent any dying reprisals on his part.

I got my wish, in large part. He swayed, straightened, dropped his gun, and fell flat on his back, giving his skull a murderous crack on the concrete for good measure. He lay there and after a half dozen gushes the bright blood quit pumping strongly out of his neck.

Then came the part that was like a dying reprisal, though obviously not being directed by him as of now. And come to think of it, it may have had its good points.

The girl, who was clearly a most cool-headed cuss, snatched for his gun where he'd dropped it, to make sure she got it ahead of me. She snatched, yes—and then jerked back, letting off a sizable squeal of pain, anger, and surprise.

Where we'd seen his gun hit the concrete there was now a tiny incandescent puddle. A rill of blood snaked out from the pool around his head and touched the whitely glowing puddle and a jet of steam sizzled up.

Somehow the gun had managed to melt itself in the moment of its owner dying. Well, at any rate that showed it hadn't contained any gunpowder or ordinary chemical explosives, though I already knew it operated on other principles from the way it had been used to paralyze me. More to the point, it showed that the gun's owner was the member of a culture that believed in taking very complete precautions against its gadgets falling into the hands of strangers.

But the gun fusing wasn't quite all. As the girl and me shifted our gaze from the puddle, which was cooling fast and now glowed red like the blood—as we shifted our gaze back from the puddle to the dead man, we saw that at three points (points over where you'd expect pockets to be) his gray clothing had charred in small irregularly shaped patches from which threads of black smoke were twisting upward.

Just at that moment, so close as to make me jump in spite of years of learning to absorb shocks stoically—right at my elbow it seemed too (the girl jumped too, I may say)—a voice said, "Done a murder, hey?"

Advancing briskly around the skewily grounded plane from the direction of the cracking plant was an old geezer, a seasoned, hard-baked Deathlander if I ever saw one. He had a shock of bone-white hair, the rest of him that showed from his weathered gray clothing looked fried by the sun's rays and others to a stringy crisp, and strapped to his boots and weighing down his belt were a good dozen knives.

Not satisfied with the unnerving noise he'd made already, he went on brightly, "Neat job too, I give you credit for that, but why the hell did you have to set the guy afire?"

CHAPTER III

We are always, thanks to our human nature, potential criminals. None of us stands outside humanity's black collective shadow.

—The Undiscovered Self,
by Carl Jung

ORDINARILY scroungers who hide around on the outskirts until the killing's done and then come in to share the loot get what they deserve—wordless orders, well backed up, to be on their way at once. Sometimes they even catch an after-clap of the murder urge, if it hasn't all been expended on the first victim or victims. Yet they *will* do it, trusting I suppose to the irresistible glamor of their personalities. There were several reasons why we didn't at once give Pop this treatment.

In the first place we didn't neither of us have our distance weapons. My revolver and her dart gun were both tucked in the cave back at the edge of the freeway. And there's one bad thing about a bugger so knife-happy he lugs them around by the carload—he's generally good at tossing them. With his dozen or so knives Pop definitely outgunned us.

Second, we were both of us without the use of an arm. That's right, the both of us. My right arm still dangled like a string of sausages and I couldn't yet feel any signs of it coming un-dead. While she'd burned her fingers badly grabbing at the gun—I could see their red-splotched tips now as she pulled them out of her mouth for a second to wipe the Pilot's blood out of her eyes. All she had was her stump with the knife screwed to it. Me, I can throw a knife left-handed if I have to, but you bet I wasn't going to risk Mother that way.

Then I'd no sooner heard Pop's voice, breathy and a little high like an old man's will get, than it occurred to me that he must have been the one who had given the funny scream that had distracted the Pilot's attention and let us get him. Which incidentally made Pop a quick thinker and imaginative to boot, and meant that he'd helped on the killing.

Besides all that, Pop did not come in fawning and full of extravagant praise, as most scroungers will. He just assumed equality with us right from the start and he talked in an absolutely matter-of-fact way, neither praising nor criticizing one bit—too damn matter-of-fact and open, for that matter, to suit my taste, but then I have heard other buggers say that some old men are apt to get talkative, though I had never worked with or run into one myself. Old people are very rare in the Deathlands, as you might imagine.

So the girl and me just scowled at him but did nothing to stop him as he came along. Near us, his extra knives would be no advantage to him.

"Hum," he said, "looks a lot like a guy I murdered five years back down Los Alamos way. Same silver monkey suit and almost as tall. Nice chap too—was trying to give me something for a fever I'd faked. That his gun melted? My man didn't smoke after I gave him his quietus, but then it turned out he didn't have any metal on him. I wonder if this chap—" He started to kneel down by the body.

"Hands off, Pop!" I gritted at him. That was how we started calling him Pop.

"Why sure, sure," he said, staying there on one knee. "I won't lay a finger on him. It's just that I've heard the Alamosers have it rigged so that any metal they're carrying melts when they die, and I was wondering about this boy. But he's all yours, friend. By the way, what's your name, friend?"

"Ray," I snarled. "Ray Baker." I think the main reason I told him was that I didn't want him calling me "friend" again. "You talk too much, Pop."

"I suppose I do, Ray," he agreed. "What's your name, lady?"

The girl just sort of hissed at him and he grinned at me as if to say, "Oh, women!" Then he said, "Why don't you go through his pockets, Ray? I'm real curious."

"Shut up," I said, but I felt that he'd put me on the spot just the same. I was curious about the guy's pockets myself, of course, but I was also wondering if Pop was alone or if he had somebody with him, and whether there was anybody else in the plane or not—things like that, too many things. At the same time I didn't want to let on to Pop how useless my right arm was—if I'd just get a twinge of feeling in that arm, I knew I'd feel a lot more confident fast. I knelt down across the body from him, started to lay Mother aside and then hesitated.

The girl gave me an encouraging look, as if to say, "I'll take care of the old geezer." On the strength of her look I put down Mother and started to pry open the Pilot's left hand, which was clenched in a fist that looked a mite too big to have nothing inside it.

The girl started to edge behind Pop, but he caught the movement right away and looked at her with a grin that was so knowing and yet so friendly, and yet so pitying at the same time—with the pity of the old pro for even the seasoned amateur—that in her place I think I'd have blushed myself, as she did now . . . through the streaks of the Pilot's blood.

"You don't have to worry none about me, lady," he said, running a hand through his white hair and incidentally touching the pommel of one of the two knives strapped high on the back of his jacket so he could reach one over either shoulder. "I quit murdering some years back. It got to be too much of a strain on my nerves."

"Oh yeah?" I couldn't help saying as I pried up the Pilot's index finger and started on the next. "Then why the stab-factory, Pop?"

"Oh you mean those," he said, glancing down at his knives. "Well, the fact is, Ray, I carry them to impress buggers dumber than you and the lady here. Anybody wants to think I'm still a practicing murderer I got no objections. Matter of sentiment, too, I just hate to part with them—they bring back important memories. And then—you won't believe this, Ray, but I'm going to tell you just the same—guys just up and give me their knives and I doubly hate to part with a gift."

I wasn't going to say "Oh yeah?" again or "Shut up!" either, though I certainly wished I could turn off Pop's spigot, or thought I did. Then I felt a painful tingling shoot down my right arm. I smiled at Pop and said, "Any other reasons?"

"Yep," he said. "Got to shave and I might as well do it in style. A new blade every day in the fortnight is twice as good as the old ads. You know, it makes you keep a knife in fine shape if you shave with it. What you got there, Ray?"

"You were wrong, Pop," I said. "He did have some metal on him that didn't melt."

I held up for them to see the object I'd extracted from his left fist: a bright steel cube measuring about an inch across each side, but it felt lighter than if it were solid metal. Five of the faces looked absolutely bare. The sixth had a round button recessed in it.

From the way they looked at it neither Pop nor the girl had the faintest idea of what it was. I certainly hadn't.

"Had he pushed the button?" the girl asked. Her voice was throaty but unexpectedly refined, as if she'd done no talking at all, not even to herself, since coming to the Deathlands and so retained the cultured intonations she'd had earlier, whenever and wherever that had been. It gave me a funny feeling, of course, because they were the first words I'd heard her speak.

"Not from the way he was holding it," I told her. "The button was pointed up toward his thumb but the thumb was on the outside of his fingers." I felt an unexpected satisfaction at having expressed myself so clearly and I told myself not to get childish.

The girl slitted her eyes. "Don't you push it, Ray," she said.

"Think I'm nuts?" I told her, meanwhile sliding the cube into the smaller pocket of my pants, where it fit tight and wouldn't turn sideways and the button maybe get pressed by accident. The tingling in my right arm was almost unbearable now, but I was getting control over the muscles again.

"Pushing that button," I added, "might melt what's left of the plane, or blow us all up." It never hurts to emphasize that you may have another weapon in your possession, even if it's just a suicide bomb.

"There was a man pushed another button once," Pop said softly and reflectively. His gaze went far out over the Deathlands and took in a good half of the horizon and he slowly shook his head. Then his face brightened. "Did you know, Ray," he said, "that I actually met that man? Long afterwards. You don't believe me, I know, but I actually did. Tell you about it some other time."

I almost said, "Thanks, Pop, for sparing me at least for a while," but I was afraid that would set him off again. Besides, it wouldn't have been quite true. I've heard other buggers tell the yarn of how they met (and invariably rubbed out) the actual guy who pushed the button or buttons that set the fusion missiles blasting toward their targets, but I felt a sudden curiosity as to what Pop's version of the yarn would be. Oh well, I could ask him some other time, if we both lived that long. I started to check the Pilot's pockets. My right hand could help a little now.

"Those look like mean burns you got there, lady," I heard Pop tell the girl. He was right. There were blisters easy to see on three of the fingertips. "I've got some salve that's pretty good," he went on, "and some clean cloth. I could put on a bandage for you if you wanted. If your hand started to feel poisoned you could always tell Ray here to slip a knife in me."

Pop was a cute gasser, you had to admit. I reminded myself that it was Pop's business to play up to the both of us, charm being the secret weapon of all scroungers.

The girl gave a harsh little laugh. "Very well," she said, "but we will use my salve, I know it works for me." And she started to lead Pop to where we'd hidden our things.

"I'll go with you," I told them, standing up.

It didn't look like we were going to have any more murders today—Pop had got through the preliminary ingratiations pretty well and the girl and me had had our catharsis—but that would be no excuse for any such stupidity as letting the two of them get near my .38.

Strolling to the cave and back I eased the situation a bit more by saying, "That scream you let off, Pop, really helped. I don't know what gave you the idea, but thanks."

"Oh that," he said. "Forget about it."

"I won't," I told him. "You may say you've quit killing, but helped on a do-in today."

"Ray," he said a little solemnly, "if it'll make you feel any happier, I'll take a bit of the responsibility for every murder that's been done since the beginning of time."

I looked at him for a while. Then, "Pop, you're not by any chance the religious type?" I asked suddenly.

"Lord, no," he told us.

That struck me as a satisfactory answer. God preserve me from the religious type! We have quite a few of those in the Deathlands. It generally means that they try to convert you to something before they kill you. Or sometimes afterwards.

We completed our errands. I felt a lot more secure with Old Financier's Friend strapped to my middle. Mother is wonderful but she is not enough.

I dawdled over inspecting the Pilot's pockets, partly to give my right hand time to come back all the way. And to tell the truth I didn't much enjoy the job—a corpse, especially such a handsome cadaver as this, just didn't go with Pop's brand of light patter.

Pop did up the girl's hand in high style, bandaging each finger separately and then persuading her to put on a big left-hand work glove he took out of his small pack.

"Lost the right," he explained, "which was the only one I ever used anyway. Never knew until now why I kept this. How does it feel, Alice?"

I might have known he'd worm her name out of her. It occurred to me that Pop's ideas of scrounging might extend to Alice's favors. The urge doesn't die out when you get old, they tell me. Not completely.

He'd also helped her replace the knife on her stump with the hook.

By that time I'd poked into all the Pilot's pockets I could get at without stripping him and found nothing but three irregularly shaped blobs of metal, still hot to the touch. Under the charred spots, of course.

I didn't want the job of stripping him. Somebody else could do a little work, I told myself. I've been bothered by bodies before (as who hasn't, I suppose?) but this one was really beginning to make me sick. Maybe I was cracking up, it occurred to me. Murder is a very wearing business, as all Deathlanders know, and although some crack earlier than others, all crack in the end.

I must have been showing how I was feeling because, "Cheer up, Ray," Pop said. "You and Alice have done a big murder—I'd say the subject was six foot ten—so you ought to be happy. You've drawn a blank on his pockets but there's still the plane."

"Yeah, that's right," I said, brightening a little. "There's still the stuff in the plane." I knew there were some items I couldn't hope for, like .38 shells, but there'd be food and other things.

"Nuh-uh," Pop corrected me. "I said *the plane*. You may have thought it's wrecked, but I don't. Have you taken a real gander at it? It's worth doing, believe me."

I jumped up. My heart was suddenly pounding. I was glad of an excuse to get away from the body, but there was a lot more in my feelings than that. I was filled with an excitement to which I didn't want to give a name because it would make the let-down too great.

One of the wide stubby wings of the plane, raking downward so that its tip almost touched the concrete, had hidden the undercarriage of the fuselage from our view. Now, coming around the wing, I saw that *there was no undercarriage.*

I had to drop to my hands and knees and scan around with my cheek next to the concrete before I'd believe it. *The "wrecked" plane was at all points at least six inches off the ground.*

I got to my feet again. I was shaking, I wanted to talk but I couldn't. I grabbed the leading edge of the wing to stop from falling. The whole body of the plane gave a fraction of an inch and then resisted my leaning weight with lazy power, just like a gyroscope.

"Antigravity," I croaked, though you couldn't have heard me two feet. Then my voice came back. "Pop, Alice! They got antigravity! Antigravity—and it's working!"

Alice had just come around the wing and was facing me. She was shaking too and her face was white like I knew mine was. Pop was politely standing off a little to one side, watching us curiously, "Told you you'd won a real prize," he said in his matter-of-fact way.

Alice wet her lips. "Ray," she said, "we can get away."

Just those four words, but they did it. Something in me unlocked— no, exploded describes it better.

"We can go places!" I almost shouted.

"Beyond the dust," she said. "Mexico City. South America!" She was forgetting the Deathlander's cynical article of belief that the dust never ends, but then so was I. It makes a difference whether or not you've got a means of doing something.

"Rio!" I topped her with. "The Indies. Hong Kong. Bombay. Egypt. Bermuda. The French Riviera!"

"Bullfights and clean beds," she burst out with. "Restaurants. Swimming pools. Bathrooms!"

"Skindiving," I took it up with, as hysterical as she was. "Road races and roulette tables."

"Bentleys and Porsches!"

"Aircoups and DC4s and Comets!"

"Martinis and hashish and ice cream sodas!"

"Hot food! Fresh coffee! Gambling, smoking, dancing, music, drinks!" I was going to add *women,* but then I thought of how hard-bitten little Alice would look beside the dream creatures I had in mind. I tactfully suppressed the word but I filed the idea away.

I don't think either of us knew exactly what we were saying. Alice in particular I don't believe was old enough to have experienced almost any of the things the words referred to. They were mysterious symbols of long-interdicted delights spewing out of us.

"Ray," Alice said, hurrying to me, "let's get aboard."

"Yes," I said eagerly and then I saw a little problem. The door to the plane was a couple of feet above our heads. Whoever hoisted himself up first—or got hoisted up, as would have to be the case with Alice on account of her hand—would be momentarily at the other's mercy. I guess it occurred to Alice too because she stopped and looked at me. It was a little like the old teaser about the fox, the goose, and the corn.

Maybe, too, we were both a little scared the plane was booby-trapped.

Pop solved the problem in the direct way I might have expected of him by stepping quietly between us, giving a light leap, catching hold of the curving sill, chinning himself on it, and scrambling up into the plane so quickly that we'd hardly have had time to do anything about it if we'd wanted to. Pop couldn't be much more than a bantamweight, even with all his knives. The plane sagged an inch and then swung up again.

As Pop disappeared from view I backed off, reaching for my .38, but a moment later he stuck out his head and grinned down at us, resting his elbows on the sill.

"Come on up," he said. "It's quite a place. I promise not to push any buttons 'til you get here, though there's whole regiments of them."

I grinned back at Pop and gave Alice a boost up. She didn't like it, but she could see it had to be her next. She hooked onto the sill and Pop caught hold of her left wrist below the big glove and heaved.

Then it was my turn. I didn't like it. I didn't like the idea of those two buggers poised above me while my hands were helpless on the sill. But I thought *Pop's a nut. You can trust a nut, at least a little ways, though you can't trust nobody else.* I heaved myself up. It was strange to feel the plane giving and then bracing itself like something alive. It seemed to have no trouble accepting our combined weight, which after all was hardly more than half again the Pilot's.

Inside the cabin was pretty small but as Pop had implied, oh my! Everything looked soft and smoothly curved, like you imagine your insides being, and almost everything was a restfully dull silver. The general shape of it was something like the inside of an egg. Forward, which was the larger end, were a couple of screens and a wide view-port and some small dials and the button brigades Pop had mentioned, lined up like blank typewriter keys but enough for writing Chinese.

Just aft of the instrument panel were two very comfortable look-ing strange low seats. They seemed to be facing backwards until I realized they were meant to be knelt into. The occupant, I could see, would sort of sprawl forward, his hands free for button-pushing and such. There were spongy chinrests.

Aft was a tiny instrument panel and a kind of sideways seat, not nearly so fancy. The door by which we'd entered was to the side, a little aft.

I didn't see any indications of cabinets or fixed storage spaces of any kinds, but somehow stuck to the walls here and there were quite a few smooth blobby packages, mostly dull silver too, some large, some small—valises and handbags, you might say.

All in all, it was a lovely cabin and, more than that, it seemed lived in. It looked as if it had been shaped for, and maybe by one man. It had a personality you could feel, a strong but warm personality of its own.

Then I realized whose personality it was. I almost got sick—so close to it I started telling myself it must be something antigravity did to your stomach.

But it was all too interesting to let you get sick right away. Pop was poking into two of the large mound-shaped cases that were sitting loose and open on the right-hand seat, as if ready for emergency use. One had a folded something with straps on it that was probably a parachute. The second had I judged a thousand or more of the inch cubes such as I'd pried out of the Pilot's hand, all neatly stacked in a cubical box inside the soft outer bag. You could see the one-cube gap where he'd taken the one.

I decided to take the rest of the bags off the walls and open them, if I could figure out how. The others had the same idea, but Alice had to take off her hook and put on her pliers, before she could make progress. Pop helped her. There was room enough for us to do these things without crowding each other too closely.

By the time Alice was set to go I'd discovered the trick of getting the bags off. You couldn't pull them away from the wall no matter what force you used, at least I couldn't, and you couldn't even slide them straight along the walls, but if you just gave them a gentle counterclockwise twist they came off like nothing. Twisting them clockwise glued them back on. It was very strange, but I told myself that if these boys could generate antigravity fields they could create screwy fields of other sorts.

It also occurred to me to wonder if "these boys" came from Earth. The Pilot had looked human enough, but these accomplishments didn't—not by my standards for human achievement in the Age of the Deaders. At any rate I had to admit to myself that my pet term "cultural queer" did not describe to my own satisfaction members of a culture which could create things like this cabin. Not that I liked making the admission. It's hard to admit an exception to a pet gripe against things.

The excitement of getting down and opening the Christmas packages saved me from speculating too much along these or any other lines.

I hit a minor jackpot right away. In the same bag were a compass, a catalytic pocket lighter, a knife with a saw-tooth back edge that made my affection for Mother waver, a dust mask, what looked like a compact water-filtration unit, and several other items adding up to a deluxe Deathlands Survival Kit.

There were some goggles in the kit I didn't savvy until I put them on and surveyed the landscape out the viewport. A nearby dust drift I knew to be hot glowed green as death in the slightly smoky lenses. Wow! Those specs had Geiger counters beat a mile and I privately bet myself they worked at night. I stuck them in my pocket quick.

We found bunches of tiny electronics parts—I think they were; spools of magnetic tape, but nothing to play it on; reels of very narrow film with frames much too small to see anything at all unmagnified; about three thousand cigarettes in unlabeled transparent packs of twenty—we lit up quick, using my new lighter; a picture book that didn't make much sense because the views might have been of tissue sections or starfields, we couldn't quite decide, and there were no captions to help; a thin book with ricepaper pages covered with Chinese characters—that was a puzzler; a thick book with nothing but columns of figures, all zeros and ones and nothing else; some tiny chisels; and a mouth organ. Pop, who'd make a point of just helping in the hunt, appropriated that last item—I might have known he would, I told myself. Now we could expect "Turkey in the Straw" at odd moments.

Alice found a whole bag of what were women's things judging from the frilliness of the garments included. She set aside some squeeze-packs and little gadgets and elastic items right away, but she didn't take any of the clothes. I caught her measuring some kind of transparent chemise against herself when she thought we weren't looking; it was for a girl maybe six sizes bigger.

And we found food. Cans of food that was heated up inside by the time you got the top rolled off, though the outside could still be cool to the touch. Cans of boneless steak, boneless chops, cream soup, peas, carrots, and fried potatoes—they weren't labeled at all but you could generally guess the contents from the shape of the can. Eggs that heated when you touched them and were soft-boiled evenly and barely firm by the time you had the shell broke. And small plastic bottles of strong coffee that heated up hospitably too—in this case the tops did a five-second hesitation in the middle of your unscrewing them.

At that point as you can imagine we let the rest of the packages go and had ourselves a feast. The food ate even better than it smelled. It was real hard for me not to gorge.

Then as I was slurping down my second bottle of coffee I happened to look out the viewport and see the Pilot's body and the darkening puddle around it and the coffee began to taste, well, not bad, but sickening. I don't think it was guilty conscience. Deathlanders outgrow those if they ever have them to start with; loners don't keep consciences—it takes cultures to give you those and make them work. Artistic inappropriateness is the closest I can come to describing what bothered me. Whatever it was, it made me feel lousy for a minute.

About the same time Alice did an odd thing with the last of *her* coffee. She slopped it on a rag and used it to wash her face. I guess she'd caught a reflection of herself with the blood smears. She didn't eat any more after that either. Pop kept on chomping away, a slow feeder and appreciative.

To be doing something I started to inspect the instrument panel and right away I was all excited again. The two screens were what got me. They showed shadowy maps, one of North America, the other of the World. The first one was a whole lot like the map I'd been imagining earlier—faint colors marked the small "civilized" areas including one in Eastern Canada and another in Upper Michigan that must be "countries" I didn't know about, and the Deathlands were real dark just as I'd always maintained they should be!

South of Lake Michigan was a brightly luminous green point that must be where we were, I decided. And for some reason the colored areas representing Los Alamos and Atlantic Highlands were glowing brighter than the others—they had an active luminosity. Los Alamos was blue, Atla-Hi violet. Los Alamos was shown having more territory than I expected. Savannah Fortress for that matter was a whole *lot* bigger than I'd have made it, pushing out pseudopods west and northeast along the coast, though its red didn't have the extra glow. But its growth-pattern reeked of imperialism.

The World screen showed dim color patches too, but for the moment I was more interested in the other.

The button armies marched right up to the lower edge of the screens and right away I got the crazy hunch that they were connected with spots on the map. Push the button for a certain spot and the plane would go there! Why, one button even seemed to have a faint violet nimbus around it (or else my eyes were going bad) as if to say, "Push me and we go to Atlantic Highlands."

A crazy notion as I say and no sensible way to handle a plane's navigation according to any standards I could imagine, but then as I've also said this plane didn't seem to be designed according to any standards but rather in line with one man's ideas, including his whims.

At any rate that was my hunch about the buttons and the screens. It tantalized rather than helped, for the only button that seemed to be marked in any way was the one (guessing by color) for Atlantic Highlands, and I certainly didn't want to go there. Like Alamos, Atla-Hi has the reputation for being a mysteriously dangerous place. Not openly mean and death-on-Deathlanders like Walla-Walla or Porter, but buggers who swing too close to Atla-Hi have a way of never turning up again. You never expect to see again two out of three buggers who pass in the night, but for three out of three to keep disappearing is against statistics.

Alice was beside me now, scanning things over too, and from the way she frowned and what not I gathered she had caught my hunch and also shared my puzzlement.

Now was the time, all right, when we needed an instruction manual and not one in Chinese neither!

Pop swallowed a mouthful and said, "Yep, now'd be a good time to have him back for a minute, to explain things a bit. Oh, don't take offense, Ray, I know how it was for you and for you too, Alice. I know the both of you *had to* murder him, it wasn't a matter of free choice, it's the way us Deathlanders are built. Just the same, it'd be nice to have a way of killing 'em and keeping them on hand at the same time. I remember feeling that way after murdering the Alamoser I told you about. You see, I come down with the very fever I'd faked and almost died of it, while the man who could have cured me easy wouldn't do nothing but perfume the landscape with the help of a gang of anaerobic bacteria. Stubborn single-minded cuss!"

The first part of that oration started up my sickness again and irked me not a little. Dammit, what right had Pop to talk about how all us Deathlanders *had to* kill (which was true enough and by itself would have made me cotten to him) if as he'd claimed earlier *he'd* been able to quit killing? Pop was an old hypocrite, I told myself—he'd helped murder the Pilot, he'd admitted as much—and Alice and me'd be better off if we bedded the both of them down together. But then the second part of what Pop said so made me want to feel pleasantly sorry for myself and laugh at the same time that I forgave the old geezer. Practically everything Pop said had that reassuring touch of insanity about it.

So it was Alice who said, "Shut up, Pop"—and rather casually at that—and she and me went on to speculate and then to argue about which buttons we ought to push, if any and in what order.

"Why not just start anywhere and keep pushing 'em one after another?—you're going to have to eventually, may as well start now," was Pop's light-hearted contribution to the discussion. "Got to take some chances in this life." He was sitting in the back seat and still nibbling away like a white-topped mangy old squirrel.

Of course Alice and me knew more than that. We kept making guesses as to how the buttons worked and then backing up our guesses with hot language. It was a little like two savages trying to decide how to play chess by looking at the pieces. And then the old escape-to-paradise theme took hold of us again and we studied the colored blobs on the World screen, trying to decide which would have the fanciest accommodations for blase ex-murderers. On the North America screen too there was an intriguing pink patch in southern Mexico that seemed to take in old Mexico City and Acapulco too.

"Quit talking and start pushing," Pop prodded us. "This way you're getting nowhere fast. I can't stand hesitation, it riles my nerves."

Alice thought you ought to push ten buttons at once, using both hands, and she was working out patterns for me to try. But I was off on a kick about how we should darken the plane to see if any of the other buttons glowed beside the one with the Atla-Hi violet.

"Look here, you killed a big man to get this plane," Pop broke in, coming up behind me. "Are you going to use it for discussion groups or are you going to fly it?"

"Quiet," I told him. I'd got a new hunch and was using the dark glasses to scan the instrument panel. They didn't show anything.

"Dammit, I can't stand this any more," Pop said and reached a hand and arm between us and brought it down on about fifty buttons, I'd judge.

The other buttons just went down and up, but the Atla-Hi button went down and stayed down.

The violet blob of Atla-Hi on the screen got even brighter in the next few moments.

The door closed with a tiny thud.

We took off.

CHAPTER IV

Any man who deals in murder, must have very incorrect ways of thinking, and truly inaccurate principles.

—*Thomas de Quincey in*
Murder Considered as One of the Fine Arts

For that matter we took off *fast* with the plane swinging to beat hell. Alice and me was in the two kneeling seats and we hugged them tight, but Pop was loose and sort of rattled around the cabin for a while—and serve him right!

On one of the swings I caught a glimpse of the seven dented gas tanks, looking like dull crescents from this angle through the orange haze and getting rapidly smaller as they hazed out.

After a while the plane levelled off and quit swinging, and a while after that my image of the cabin quit swinging too. Once again I just managed to stave off the vomits, this time the vomits from natural causes. Alice looked very pale around the gills and kept her face buried in the chin-rest of her chair.

Pop ended up right in our faces, sort of spread-eagled against the instrument panel. In getting himself off it he must have braced his hands against half the buttons at one time or another and I noticed that none of them went down a fraction. They were *locked*. It had probably happened automatically when the Atla-Hi button got pushed.

I'd have stopped him messing around in that apish way, but with the ultra-queasy state of my stomach I lacked all ambition and was happy just not to be smelling him so close.

45

I still wasn't taking too great an interest in things as I idly watched the old geezer rummaging around the cabin for something that got misplaced in the shake-up. Eventually he found it—a small almond-shaped can. He opened it. Sure enough it turned out to have almonds in it. He fitted himself in the back seat and munched them one at a time. Ish!

"Nothing like a few nuts to top off with," he said cheerfully.

I could have cut his throat even more cheerfully, but the damage had been done and you think twice before you kill a person in close quarters when you aren't absolutely sure you'll be able to dispose of the body. How did I know I'd be able to open the door? I remember philosophizing that Pop ought at least to have broke an arm so he'd be as badly off as Alice and me (though for that matter my right arm was fully recovered now) but he was all in one piece. There's no justice in events, that's for sure.

The plane ploughed along silently through the orange soup, though there was really no way to tell it was moving now—until a skewy spindle shape loomed up ahead and shot back over the viewport. I think it was a vulture. I don't know how vultures manage to operate in the haze, which ought to cancel their keen eyesight, but they do. It shot past *fast*.

Alice lifted her face out of the sponge stuff and began to study the buttons again. I heaved myself up and around a little and said, "Pop, Alice and me are going to try to work out how this plane navigates. This time we don't want no interference." I didn't say a word more about what he'd done. It never does to hash over stupidities.

"That's perfectly fine, go right ahead," he told me. "I feel calm as a kitten now we're going somewheres. That's all that ever matters with me." He chuckled a bit and added, "You got to admit I gave you and Alice something to work with," but then he had the sense to shut up tight.

We weren't so chary of pushing buttons this time, but ten minutes or so convinced us that you couldn't push any of the buttons any more, they *were* all locked down—all locked except for maybe one, which we didn't try at first for a special reason.

We looked for other controls—sticks, levers, pedals, finger-holes and the like. There weren't any. Alice went back and tried the buttons on Pop's minor console. They were locked too. Pop looked interested but didn't say a word.

We realized in a general way what had happened, of course. Pushing the Atla-Hi button had set us on some kind of irreversible automatic. I couldn't imagine the why of gimmicking a plane's controls like that, unless maybe to keep loose children or prisoners from being able to mess things up while the pilot took a snooze, but there were a lot of whys to this plane that didn't seem to have any standard answers.

The business of taking off on irreversible automatic had happened so neatly that I naturally wondered whether Pop might not know more about navigating this plane than he let on, a whole lot more in fact, and the seemingly idiotic petulance of his pushing all the buttons have been a shrewd cover for pushing the Atla-Hi button. But if Pop had been acting he'd been acting beautifully, with a serene disregard for the chances of breaking his own neck. I decided this was a possibility I could think about later and maybe act on then, after Alice and me had worked through the more obvious stuff.

The reason we hadn't tried the one button yet was that it showed a green nimbus, just like the Atla-Hi button had had a violet nimbus. Now there was no green on either of the screens except for the tiny green star that I had figured stood for the plane and it didn't make sense to go where we already were. And if it meant some other place, some place not shown on the screens, you bet we weren't going to be too quick about deciding to go there. It might not be on Earth.

Alice expressed it by saying, "My namesake was always a little too quick at responding to those DRINK ME cues."

I suppose she thought she was being cryptic, but I fooled her. "*Alice in Wonderland?*" I asked. She nodded and gave me a little smile, not at all like one of the EAT ME smiles she'd given me last evening.

It is funny how crazily happy a little touch of the intellectual past like that can make you feel—and how horribly uncomfortable a moment later.

We both started to study the North America screen again and almost at once we realized that it had changed in one small particular. The green star had twinned. Where there had been one point of green light there were now two, very close together like the double star in the handle of the Dipper. We watched it for a while. The distance between the two stars grew perceptibly greater. We watched it for a while longer, considerably longer. It became clear that the position of the more westerly star on the screen was fixed, while the more easterly star was moving east toward Atla-Hi with about the speed of the tip of the minute hand on a wrist watch (two inches an hour, say). The pattern began to make sense.

I figured it this way: the moving star must stand for the plane, the other green dot must stand for where the plane had just been. For some reason the spot on the freeway by the old cracking plant was recognized as a marked locality by the screen. Why I don't know. It reminded me of the old "X Marks the Spot" of newspaper murders, but that would be getting very fancy. Anyway the spot we'd just taken off from was so marked and in that case the button with the green nimbus . . .

"Hold tight, everybody," I said to Alice, grudgingly including Pop in my warning. "I got to try it."

I gripped my seat with my knees and one arm and pushed the green button. It pushed.

The plane swung around in a level loop, not too tight to disturb the stomach much, and steadied out again.

I couldn't judge how far we'd swung but Alice and me watched the green stars and after about a minute she said, "They're getting closer," and a little while later I said, "Yeah, for sure."

I scanned the board. The green button—the cracking-plant button, to call it that—was locked down of course. The Atla-Hi button was up, glowing violet. All the other buttons were still up and *locked up*—I tried them all again.

It was clear as day used to be. We could either go to Atla-Hi or we could go back where we'd started from. There was no third possibility.

It was a little hard to take. You think of a plane as freedom, as something that will carry you anywhere in the world you choose to go, especially any paradise, and then you find yourself worse limited than if you'd stayed on the ground—at least that was the way it was happening to us.

But Alice and me were realists. We knew it wouldn't help to wail. We were up against another of those "two" problems, the problem of two destinations, and we had to choose ours.

If we go back, I thought, *we can trek on somewhere—anywhere— richer by the loot from the plane, especially that Survival Kit. Trek on with some loot we'll mostly never understand and with the knowledge that we are leaving a plane that can fly, that we are shrinking back from an unknown adventure.*

Also if we go back there's something else we'll have to face, something we'll have to live with for a little while at least that won't be nice to live with after this cozily personal cabin, something that shouldn't bother me at all but, dammit, it does.

Alice made the decision for us and at the same time showed she was thinking about the same thing as me.

"I don't want to have to smell him, Ray," she said. "I am not going back to keep company with that filthy corpse. I'd rather anything than that." And she pushed the Atla-Hi button again and as the plane started to swing she looked at me defiantly as if to say I'd reverse the course again over her dead body.

"Don't tense up," I told her. "I want a new shake of the dice myself."

"You know, Alice," Pop said reflectively, "it was the smell of my Alamoser got to me too. I just couldn't bear it. I couldn't get away from it because my fever had me pinned down, so there was nothing left for me to do but go crazy. No Atla-Hi for me, just Bug-land. My mind died, though not my memory. By the time I'd got my strength back I'd started to be a new bugger. I didn't know no more about living than a newborn babe, except I knew I couldn't go back—go back to murdering and all that. My new mind knew that much though otherwise it was just a blank. It was all very funny."

"And then I suppose," Alice cut in, her voice corrosive with sarcasm, "you hunted up a wandering preacher, or perhaps a kindly old hermit who lived on hot manna, and he showed you the blue sky!"

"Why no, Alice," Pop said. "I told you I don't go for religion. As it happens, I hunted me up a couple of murderers, guys who were worse cases then myself but who'd wanted to quit because it wasn't getting them nowhere and who'd found, I'd heard, a way of quitting, and the three of us had a long talk together."

"And they told you the great secret of how to live in the Deathlands without killing," Alice continued acidly. "Drop the nonsense, Pop. It can't be done."

"It's hard, I'll grant you," Pop said. "You have to go crazy or something almost as bad—in fact, maybe going crazy is the easiest way. But it can be done and, in the long run, murder is even harder."

I decided to interrupt this idle chatter. Since we were now definitely headed for Atla-Hi and there was nothing to do until we got there, unless one of us got a brainstorm about the controls, it was time to start on the less obvious stuff I'd tabled in my mind.

"Why are you on this plane, Pop?" I asked sharply. "What do you figure on getting out of Alice and me?—and I don't mean the free meals."

He grinned. His teeth were white and even—plates, of course. "Why, Ray," he said, "I was just giving Alice the reason. I like to talk to murderers, practicing murderers preferred. I need to—*have* to talk to 'em, to keep myself straight. Otherwise I might start killing again and I'm not up to that any more."

"Oh, so you get your kicks at second hand, you old peeper," Alice put in but, "Quit lying, Pop," I said. "About having quit killing, for one thing. In my books, which happen to be the old books in this case, the accomplice is every bit as guilty as the man with the slicer. You helped us kill the Pilot by giving that funny scream and you know it."

"Who says I did?" Pop countered, rearing up a little. "I never said so. I just said, 'Forget it.'" He hesitated a moment, studying me. Then he said, "I wasn't the one gave that scream. In fact, I'd have stopped it if I'd been able."

"Who did then?"

Again he studied me as he hesitated. "I'm not telling," he said, settling back.

"Pop!" I said, sharp again. "Buggers who pad together tell everything."

"Oh yeah," he agreed, smiling. "I remember saying that to quite a few guys in my day. It's a very restful comradely sentiment. I killed every last one of 'em, too."

"You may have, Pop," I granted, "but we're two to one."

"So you are," he agreed softly, looking the both of us over. I knew what he was thinking—that Alice still had just her pliers on and that in these close quarters his knives were as good as my gun.

"Give me your right hand, Alice," I said. Without taking my eyes off Pop I reached the knife without a handle out of her belt and then I started to unscrew the pliers out of her stump.

"Pop," I said as I did so, "you may have quit killing for all I know. I mean you may have quit killing clean decent Deathland style. But I don't believe one bit of that guff about having to talk to murderers to keep your mind sweet. Furthermore—"

"It's true though," he interrupted. "I got to keep myself reminded of how lousy it feels to be a murderer."

"So?" I said. "Well, here's one person who believes you've got a more practical reason for being on this plane. Pop, what's the bounty Atla-Hi gives you for every Deathlander you bring in? What would it be for two live Deathlanders ? And what sort of reward would they pay for a lost plane brought in? Seems to me they might very well make you a citizen for that."

"Yes, even give you your own church," Alice added with a sort of wicked gaiety. I squeezed her stump gently to tell her to let me handle it.

"Why, I guess you can believe that if you want to," Pop said and let out a soft breath. "Seems to me you need a lot of coincidences and happenstances to make that theory hold water, but you sure can believe it if you want to. I got no way, Ray, to prove to you I'm telling the truth except to say I am."

"Right," I said and then I threw the next one at him real fast. "What's more, Pop, weren't you traveling in this plane to begin with? That cuts a happenstance. Didn't you hop out while we were too busy with the Pilot to notice and just *pretend* to be coming from the cracking plant? Weren't the buttons locked because you were the Pilot's prisoner?"

Pop creased his brow thoughtfully. "It could have been that way," he said at last. "Could have been—according to the evidence as you saw it. It's quite a bright idea, Ray. I can almost see myself skulking in this cabin, while you and Alice—"

"You were skulking somewhere," I said. I finished screwing in the knife and gave Alice back her hand. "I'll repeat it, Pop," I said. "We're two to one. You'd better talk."

"Yes," Alice added, disregarding my previous hint. "You may have given up fighting, Pop, but I haven't. Not fighting, nor killing, nor anything in between those two. Any least thing." My girl was being her most pantherish.

"Now who says I've given up *fighting*?" Pop demanded, rearing a little again. "You people assume too much, it's a dangerous habit. Before we have any trouble and somebody squawks about me cheating, let's get one thing straight. If anybody jumps me I'll try to disable them, I'll try to hurt them in any way short of killing, and that means hamstringing and rabbit-punching and everything else. Every least thing, Alice. And if they happen to die while I'm honestly just trying to hurt them in a way short of killing, then I won't grieve too much. My conscience will be reasonably clear. Is that understood?"

I had to admit that it was. Pop might be lying about a lot of things, but I just didn't believe he was lying about this. And I already knew Pop was quick for his age and strong enough. If Alice and me jumped him now there'd be blood let six different ways. You can't jump a man who has a dozen knives easy to hand and not expect that to happen, two to one or not. We'd get him in the end but it would be gory.

"And now," Pop said quietly, "I *will* talk a little if you don't mind. Look here, Ray . . . Alice . . . the two of you are confirmed murderers, I know you wouldn't tell me nothing different, and being such you both know that there's nothing in murder in the long run. It satisfies a hunger and maybe gets you a little loot and it lets you get on to the next killing. But that's all, absolutely all. Yet you got to do it because it's the way you're built. The urge is there, it's an overpowering urge, and you got nothing to oppose it with. You feel the Big Grief and the Big Resentment, the dust is eating at your bones, you can't stand the city squares—the Porterites and Mantenors and such—because you know they're whistling in the dark and it's a dirty tune, so you go on killing. But if there were a decent practical way to quit, you'd take it. At least I think you would. When you still thought this plane could take you to Rio or Europe you felt that way, didn't you? You weren't planning to go there as murderers, were you? You were going to leave your trade behind."

It was pretty quiet in the cabin for a couple of seconds. Then Alice's thin laugh sliced the silence. "We were dreaming then," she said. "We were out of our heads. But now you're talking about practical things, as you say. What do you expect us to do if we quit our trade, as you call it—go into Walla Walla or Ouachita and give ourselves up? I might lose more than my right hand at Ouachita this time—that was just on suspicion."

"Or Atla-Hi," I added meaningfully. "Are you expecting us to admit we're murderers when we get to Atla-Hi, Pop?"

The old geezer smiled and thinned his eyes. "Now that wouldn't accomplish much, would it? Most places they'd just string you up, maybe after tickling your pain nerves a bit, or if it was Manteno they might put you in a cage and feed you slops and pray over you, and would that help you or anybody else? If a man or woman quits killing there's a lot of things he's got to straighten out—first his own mind and feelings, next he's got to do what he can to make up for the murders he's done—help the next of kin if any and so on—then he's got to carry the news to other killers who haven't heard it yet. He's got no time to waste being hanged. Believe me, he's got work lined up for him, work that's got to be done mostly in the Deathlands, and it's the sort of work the city squares can't help him with one bit, because they just don't understand us murderers and what makes us tick. We have to do it ourselves."

"Hey, Pop," I cut in, getting a little interested in the argument (there wasn't anything else to get interested in until we got to Atla-Hi or Pop let down his guard), "I dig you on the city squares (I call 'em cultural queers) and what sort of screwed-up fatheads they are, but just the same for a man to quit killing he's got to quit lone-wolfing it. He's got to belong to a community, he's got to have a culture of some sort, no matter how disgusting or nutsy."

"Well," Pop said, "don't us Deathlanders have a culture? With customs and folkways and all the rest? A very tight little culture, in fact. Nutsy as all get out, of course, but that's one of the beauties of it."

"Oh sure," I granted him, "but it's a culture based on murder and devoted wholly to murder. Murder is our way of life. That gets your argument nowhere, Pop."

"Correction," he said. "Or rather, re-interpretation." And now for a little while his voice got less old-man harsh and yet bigger somehow, as if it were more than just Pop talking. "Every culture," he said, "is a way of growth as well as a way of life, because the first law of life is growth. Our Deathland culture is devoted to growing *through* murder *away from* murder. That's my thought. It's about the toughest way of growth anybody was ever asked to face up to, but it's a way of growth just the same. A lot bigger and fancier cultures never could figure out the answer to the problem of war and killing—*we* know that, all right, we inhabit their grandest failure. Maybe us Deathlanders, working with murder every day, unable to pretend that it isn't part of every one of us, unable to put it out of our minds like the city squares do—maybe us Deathlanders are the ones to do that little job."

"But hell, Pop," I objected, getting excited in spite of myself, "even if we got a culture here in the Deathlands, a culture that can grow, it ain't a culture that can deal with repentant murderers. In a *real* culture a murderer feels guilty and confesses and then he gets hanged or imprisoned a long time and that squares things for him and everybody. You need religion and courts and hangmen and screws and all the rest of it. I don't think it's enough for a man just to say he's sorry and go around gladhanding other killers—*that* isn't going to be enough to wipe out his sense of guilt."

Pop squared his eyes at mine. "Are you so fancy that you have to have a sense of guilt, Ray?" he demanded. "Can't you just see when something's lousy? A sense of guilt's a luxury. Of course it's not enough to say you're sorry—you're going to have to spend a good part of the rest of your life making up for what you've done ... and what you will do, too! But about hanging and prisons—was it ever proved those were the right thing for murderers? As for religion now—some of us who've quit killing are religious and a lot of us (me included) aren't; and some of the ones that are religious figure (maybe because there's no way for them to get hanged) that they're damned eternally—but that doesn't stop them doing good work. I ask you now, is any little thing like being damned eternally a satisfactory excuse for behaving like a complete rat?"

That did it, somehow. That last statement of Pop's appealed so much to me and was completely crazy at the same time, that I couldn't help warming up to him. Don't get me wrong, I didn't really fall for his line of chatter at all, but I found it fun to go along with it— so long as the plane was in this shuttle situation and we had nothing better to do.

Alice seemed to feel the same way. I guess any bugger that could
kid religion the way Pop could got a little silver star in her books.
Bronze, anyway.

Right away the atmosphere got easier. To start with we asked
Pop to tell us about this "us" he kept mentioning and he said it was
some dozens (or hundreds—nobody had accurate figures) of killers who'd quit and went nomading around the Deathlands trying to
recruit others and help those who wanted to be helped. They had
semi-permanent meeting places where they tried to get together
at pre-arranged dates, but mostly they kept on the go, by twos and
threes or—more rarely—alone. They were all men so far, at least
Pop hadn't heard of any women members, but—he assured Alice
earnestly—he would personally guarantee that there would be no
objections to a girl joining up. They had recently taken to calling
themselves Murderers Anonymous, after some pre-war organization
Pop didn't know the original purpose of. Quite a few of them had
slipped and gone back to murdering again, but some of these had
come back after a while, more determined than ever to make a go
of it.

"We welcomed 'em, of course," Pop said. "We welcome everybody.
Everybody that's a genuine murderer, that is, and says he wants to
quit. Guys that aren't blooded yet we draw the line at, no matter how
fine they are."

Also, "We have a lot of fun at our meetings," Pop assured us. "You
never saw such high times. Nobody's got a right to go glooming
around or pull a long face just because he's done a killing or two.
Religion or no religion, pride's a sin."

Alice and me ate it all up like we was a couple of kids and Pop was
telling us fairy tales. That's what it all was, of course, a fairy tale—a
crazy mixed-up fairy tale. Alice and me knew there could be no fellowship of Deathlanders like Pop was describing—it was impossible
as blue sky—but it gave us a kick to pretend to ourselves for a while
to believe in it.

Pop could talk forever, apparently, about murder and murderers and he had a bottomless bag of funny stories on the same topic and character vignettes—the murderers who were forever wanting their victims to understand and forgive them, the ones who thought of themselves as little kings with divine rights of dispensing death, the ones who insisted on laying down (chastely) beside their finished victims and playing dead for a couple of hours, the ones who weren't so chaste, the ones who could only do their killings when they were dressed a certain way (and the troubles they had with their murder costumes), the ones who could only kill people with certain traits or of a certain appearance (red-heads, say, or people who read books, or who couldn't carry tunes, or who used bad language), the ones who always mixed sex and murder and the ones who believed that murder was contaminated by the least breath of sex, the sticklers and the Sloppy Joes, the artists and the butchers, the ax- and stiletto-types, the *compulsives* and the *repulsives*—honestly, Pop's portraits from life added up to a Dance of Death as good as anything the Middle Ages ever produced and they ought to have been illustrated like those by some great artist. Pop told us a lot about his own killings too. Alice and me was interested, but neither of us wasn't tempted into making parallel revelations about ourselves. Your private life's your own business, I felt, as close as your guts, and no joke's good enough to justify revealing a knot of it.

Not that we talked about nothing but murder while we were bulleting along toward Atla-Hi. The conversation was free-wheeling and we got onto all sorts of topics. For instance, we got to talking about the plane and how it flew itself—or levitated itself, rather. I said it must generate an antigravity field that was keyed to the body of the plane but nothing else, so that *we* didn't feel lighter, nor any of the objects in the cabin—it just worked on the dull silvery metal—and I proved my point by using Mother to shave a little wisp of metal off the edge of the control board. The curlicue stayed in the air wherever you put it and when you moved it you could feel the faintest sort of gyroscopic resistance. It was very strange.

Pop pointed out it was a little like magnetism. A germ riding on an iron filing that was traveling toward the pole of a big magnet wouldn't feel the magnetic pull—it wouldn't be operating on him, only on the iron—but just the same the germ'd be carried along with the filing and feel its acceleration and all, provided he could hold on—but for that purpose you could imagine a tiny cabin in the filing. "That's what we are," Pop added. "Three germs, jumbo size."

Alice wanted to know why an antigravity plane should have even the stubbiest wings or a jet for that matter, for we remembered now we'd noticed the tubes, and I said it was maybe just a reserve system in case the antigravity failed and Pop guessed it might be for extra-fast battle maneuvering or even for operating outside the atmosphere (which hardly made sense, as I proved to him).

"If we're a battle plane, where's our guns?" Alice asked. None of us had an answer.

We remembered the noise the plane had made before we saw it. It must have been using its jets then. "And do you suppose," Pop asked, "that it was something from the antigravity that made electricity flare out of the top of the cracking plant? Like to have scared the pants off me!" No answer to that either.

Now was a logical time, of course, to ask Pop what he knew about the cracking plant and just who had done the scream if not him, but I figured he still wouldn't talk; as long as we were acting friendly there was no point in spoiling it.

We guessed around a little, though, about where the plane came from. Pop said Alamos, I said Atla-Hi, Alice said why not from both, why couldn't Alamos and Atla-Hi have some sort of treaty and the plane be traveling from the one to the other. We agreed it might be. At least it fitted with the Atla-Hi violet and the Alamos blue being brighter than the other colors.

"I just hope we got some sort of anti-collision radar," I said. I guessed we had, because twice we'd jogged in our course a little, maybe to clear the Alleghenies. The easterly green star was by now getting pretty close to the violet blot of Atla-Hi. I looked out at the orange soup, which was *one* thing that hadn't changed a bit so far, and I got to wishing like a baby that it wasn't there and to thinking how it blanketed the whole Earth (stars over the Riviera?—don't make me laugh!) and I heard myself asking, "Pop, did you rub out that guy that pushed the buttons for all this?"

"Nope," Pop answered without hesitation, just as if it hadn't been four hours or so since he'd mentioned the point. "Nope, Ray. Fact is I welcomed him into our little fellowship about six months back. This is *his* knife here, this horn-handle in my boot, though he never killed with it. He claimed he'd been tortured for years by the thought of the millions and millions he'd killed with blast and radiation, but now he was finding peace at last because he was where he belonged, with the murderers, and could start to do something about it. Several of the boys didn't want to let him in. They claimed he wasn't a real murderer, doing it by remote control, no matter how many he bumped off."

"I'd have been on their side," Alice said, thinning her lips.

"Yep," Pop continued, "they got real hot about it. *He* got hot too and all excited and offered to go out and kill somebody with his bare hands right off, or try to (he's a skinny little runt), if that's what he had to do to join. We argued it over, I pointed out that we let ex-soldiers count the killings they'd done in service, and that we counted poisonings and booby traps and such too—which are remote-control killings in a way—so eventually we let him in. He's doing good work. We're fortunate to have him."

"Do you think he's really the guy who pushed the buttons?" I asked Pop.

"How should I know?" Pop replied. "He claims to be."

I was going to say something about people who faked confessions to get a little easy glory, as compared to the guys who were really guilty and would sooner be chopped up than talk about it, but at that moment a fourth voice started talking in the plane. It seemed to be coming out of the violet patch on the North America screen. That is, it came from the general direction of the screen at any rate and my mind instantly tied it to the violet patch at Atla-Hi. It gave us a fright, I can tell you. Alice grabbed my knee with her pliers (she changed again), harder than she'd intended, I suppose, though I didn't let out a yip—I was too defensively frozen.

The voice was talking a language I didn't understand at all that went up and down the scale like atonal music.

"Sounds like Chinese," Pop whispered, giving me a nudge.

"It *is* Chinese. Mandarin," the screen responded instantly in the purest English—at least that was how I'd describe it. Practically Boston. "Who are you? And where is Grayl? Come in, Grayl."

I knew well enough who Grayl must be—or rather, have been. I looked at Pop and Alice. Pop grinned, maybe a mite feebly this time, I thought, and gave me a look as if to say, "*You* want to handle it?"

I cleared my throat. Then, "We've taken over for Grayl," I said to the screen.

"Oh." The screen hesitated, just barely. Then, "Do any of 'you' speak Mandarin?"

I hardly bothered to look at Pop and Alice. "No," I said.

"Oh." Again a tiny pause. "Is Grayl aboard the plane?"

"No." I said.

"Oh. Incapacitated in some way, I suppose?"

"Yes," I said, grateful for the screen's tactfulness, unintentional or not.

"But you have taken over for him?" the screen pressed.

"Yes," I said, swallowing. I didn't know what I was getting us into, things were moving too fast, but it seemed the merest sense to act cooperative.

"I'm very glad of that," the screen said with something in its tone that made me feel funny—I guess it was sincerity. Then it said, "Is the—" and hesitated, and started again with "Are the blocks aboard?"

I thought. Alice pointed at the stuff she dumped out of the other seat. I said. "There's a box with a thousand or so one-inch underweight steel cubes in it. Like a child's blocks, but with buttons in them. Alongside a box with a parachute."

"That's what I mean," the screen said and somehow, maybe because whoever was talking was trying to hide it, I caught a note of great relief.

"Look," the screen said, more rapidly now, "I don't know how much you know, but we may have to work very fast. You aren't going to be able to deliver the steel cubes to us directly. In fact you aren't going to be able to land in Atlantic Highlands at all. We're seiged in by planes and ground forces of Savannah Fortress. All our aircraft, such as haven't been destroyed, are pinned down. You're going to have to parachute the blocks to a point as near as possible to one of our ground parties that's made a sortie. We'll give you a signal. I hope it will be later—nearer here, that is—but it may be sooner. Do you know how to fight the plane you're in? Operate its armament?"

"No," I said, wetting my lip.

"Then that's the first thing I'd best teach you. Anything you see in the haze from now on will be from Savannah. You must shoot it down."

CHAPTER V

And we are here as on a darkling plain
Swept with confused alarms of struggle and flight,
Where ignorant armies clash by night.

—Dover Beach,
by Matthew Arnold

I am not going to try to describe point by point all that happened the next half hour because there was too much of it and it involved all three of us, sometimes doing different things at the same time, and although we were told a lot of things, we were seldom if ever told the why of them, and through it all was the constant impression that we were dealing with human beings (I almost left out the "human" and I'm still not absolutely sure whether I shouldn't) of vastly greater scope—and probably intelligence too—than ourselves.

And that was just the *basic* confusion, to give it a name. After a while the situation got more difficult, as I'll try to tell in due course.

To begin with, it was extremely weird to plunge from a rather leisurely confab about a fairytale fellowship of non-practicing murderers into a shooting war between a violet blob and a dark red puddle on a shadowy fluorescent map. The voice didn't throw any great shining lights on this topic, because after the first—and perhaps unguarded—revelation, we learned little more of the war between Atla-Hi and Savannah Fortress and nothing of the reasons behind it. Presumably Savannah was the aggressor, reaching out north after the conquest of Birmingham, but even that was just a guess. It is hard to describe how shadowy it all felt to me; there were some minutes while my mind kept mixing up the whole thing with what I'd read long ago about the Civil War: Savannah was Lee, Atla-Hi was Grant, and we had been dropped spang into the middle of the second Battle of the Wilderness.

Apparently the Savannah planes had some sort of needle ray as part of their armament—at any rate I was warned to watch out for "swinging lines in the haze, like straight strings of pink stars" and later told to aim at the sources of such lines. And naturally I guessed that the steel cubes must be some crucial weapon for Atla-Hi, or ammunition for a weapon, or parts for some essential instrument like a giant computer, but the voice ignored my questions on that point and didn't fall into the couple of crude conversational traps I tried to set. We were to drop the cubes when told, that was all. Pop had the box of them closed again and rigged to the parachute—he took over that job because Alice and me were busy with other things when the instructions on that came through—and he was told how to open the door of the plane for the drop (you just held your hand steadily on a point beside the door), but, as I say, that was all.

Naturally it occurred to me that once we had made the drop, Atla-Hi would have no more use for us and might simply let us be destroyed by Savannah or otherwise—perhaps *want* us to be destroyed—so that it might be wisest for us to refuse to make the drop when the signal came and hang onto those myriad steel cubes as our only bargaining point. Still, I could see no advantage to refusing *before* the signal came. I'd have liked to discuss the point with Alice and maybe Pop too, but apparently everything we said, even whispered, could be overheard by Atla-Hi. (We never did determine, incidentally, whether Atla-Hi could *see* into the cabin of the plane also. I don't believe they could, though they sure had it bugged for sound.)

All in all, we found out almost nothing about Atla-Hi. In fact, three witless germs traveling in a cabin in an iron filing wasn't a bad description of us at all. As I often say of my deductive faculties—think—shmink! But Atla-Hi (always meaning, of course, the personality behind the voice from the screen) found out all it wanted about us—and apparently knew a good deal to start with. For one thing, they must have been tracking our plane for some time, because they guessed it was on automatic and that we could reverse its course but nothing else. Though they seemed under the impression that we could reverse its course to Los Alamos, not the cracking plant. Here obviously I did get a nugget of new data, though it was just about the only one. For a moment the voice from the screen got real unguarded-anxious as it asked, "Do you know if it is true that they have stopped dying at Los Alamos, or are they merely broadcasting that to cheer us up?"

I answered, "Oh yes, they're all fine," to that, but I couldn't have made it very convincing, because the next thing I knew the voice was getting me to admit that we'd only boarded the plane somewhere in the Central Deathlands. I even had to describe the cracking plant and freeway and gas tanks—I couldn't think of a lie that mightn't get us into as much trouble as the truth—and the voice said, "Oh, did Grayl stay there?" and I said, "Yes," and braced myself to do some more admitting, or some heavy lying, as the inspiration took me.

But the voice continued to skirt around the question of what exactly had happened to Grayl. I guess they knew well enough we'd bumped him off, but didn't bring it up because they needed our cooperation—they were handling us like children or savages, you see.

One pretty amazing point—Atla-Hi apparently knew something about Pop's fairy-tale fellowship of non-practicing murderers, because when he had to speak up, while he was getting instructions on preparing the stuff for the drop, the voice said, "Excuse me, but you sound like one of those M. A. boys."

Murderers Anonymous, Pop had said some of their boys called their unorganized organization.

"Yep, I am," Pop admitted uncomfortably.

"Well, a word of advice then, or perhaps I only mean gossip," the screen said, for once getting on a side track. "Most of our people do not believe you are serious about it, although you may think that you are. Our skeptics (which includes all but a very few of us) split quite evenly between those who think that the M. A. spirit is a terminal psychotic illusion and those who believe it is an elaborate ruse in preparation for some concerted attack on cities by Deathlanders."

"Can't say that I blame the either of them," was Pop's only comment. "I think I'm nuts myself and a murderer forever." Alice glared at him for that admission, but it seemed to do us no damage. Pop really did seem out of his depth though during this part of our adventure, more out of his depth than even Alice and me—I mean, as if he could only really function in the Deathland with Deathlanders and wanted to get anything else over quickly.

I think one reason Pop was that way was that he was feeling very intensely something I was feeling myself: a sort of sadness and bewilderment that beings as smart as the voice from the screen sounded should still be fighting wars. Murder, as you must know by now, I can understand and sympathize with deeply, but war?—no!

Oh, I can understand cultural queers fighting city squares and even get a kick out of it and whoop 'em on, but these Atla-Hi and Alamos folk seemed a different sort of cat altogether (though I'd only come to that point of view today)—the kind of cat that ought to have outgrown war or thought its way around it. Maybe Savannah Fortress had simply forced the war on them and they had to defend themselves. I hadn't contacted any Savannans—they might be as blood-simple as the Porterites. Still, I don't know that it's always a good excuse that somebody else forced you into war. That sort of justification can keep on until the end of time. But who's a germ to judge?

A minute later I was feeling doubly like a germ and a very lowly one, because the situation had just got more difficult and depressing too—the thing had happened that I said I'd tell you about in due course.

The voice was just repeating its instructions to Pop on making the drop, when it broke off of a sudden and a second voice came in, a deep voice with a sort of European accent (not Chinese, oddly)—not talking *to* us, I think, but to the first voice and overlooking or not caring that we could hear.

"*Also* tell them," the second voice said, "that we will blow them out of the sky the instant they stop obeying us! If they should hesitate to make the drop or if they should put a finger on the button that reverses their course, then—*pouf!* Such brutes understand only the language of force. *Also* warn them that the blocks are atomic grenades that will blow them out of the sky too if—"

"Dr. Kovalsky, will you permit me to point out—" the first voice interrupted, getting as close to expressing irritation as I imagine it ever allowed itself to do. Then both voices cut off abruptly and the screen was silent for ten seconds or so. I guess the first voice thought it wasn't nice for us to overhear Atla-Hi bickering with itself, even if the second voice didn't give a damn (any more than a farmer would mind the pigs overhearing him squabble with his hired man; of course this guy seemed to overlook that we were killer-pigs, but there wasn't anything we could do in that line just now except get burned up).

When the screen came on again, it was just the first voice talking once more, but it had something to say that was probably the result of a rapid conference and compromise.

"Attention, everyone! I wish to inform you that the plane in which you are traveling can be exploded—melted in the air, rather—if we activate a certain control at this end. We will *not* do so, now or subsequently, if you make the drop when we give the signal and if you remain on your present course until then. Afterwards you will be at liberty to reverse your course and escape as best you may. Let me re-emphasize that when you told me you had taken over for Grayl I accepted that assertion in full faith and still so accept it. Is that all fully understood?"

We all told him "Yes," though I don't imagine we sounded very happy about it, even Pop. However I did get that funny feeling again that the voice was being really sincere—an illusion, I supposed, but still a comforting one.

Now while all these things were going on, believe it or not, and while the plane continued to bullet through the orange haze—which hadn't shown any foreign objects in it so far, thank God, even vultures, let alone "straight strings of pink stars"—I was receiving a cram course in gunnery! (Do you wonder I don't try to tell this part of my story consecutively?)

It turned out that Alice had been brilliantly right about one thing: if you pushed some of the buttons simultaneously in patterns of five they unlocked and you could play on them like organ keys. Two sets of five keys, played properly, would rig out a sight just in front of the viewport and let you aim and fire the plane's main gun in any forward direction. There was a rearward firing gun too, that you aimed by changing over the World Screen to a rear-view TV window, but we didn't get around to mastering that one. In fact, in spite of my special talents it was all I could do to achieve a beginner's control over the main gun, and I wouldn't have managed even that except that Alice, from the thinking she'd been doing about patterns of five, was quick at understanding from the voice's descriptions which buttons were meant. She couldn't work them herself of course, what with her stump and burnt hand, but she could point them out for me.

After twenty minutes of drill I was a gunner of sorts, sprawled in the right-hand kneeling seat and intently scanning the on rushing orange haze which at last was beginning to change toward the bronze of evening. If something showed up in it I'd be able to make a stab at getting a shot in. Not that I knew what my gun fired—the voice wasn't giving away any unnecessary data.

Naturally I had asked why didn't the voice teach me to fly the plane so that I could maneuver in case of attack, and naturally the voice had told me it was out of the question—much too difficult and besides they wanted us on a known course so they could plan better for the drop and recovery. (I think maybe the voice would have given me some hints—and maybe even told me more about the steel cubes too and how much danger we were in from them—if it hadn't been for the second voice, which presumably had issued from a being who was keeping watch to make sure among other things that the first voice didn't get soft-hearted.)

So there I was being a front gunner. Actually a part of me was getting a big bang out of it—from antique Banker's Special to needle cannon (or whatever it was)—but at the same time another part of me was disgusted with the idea of acting like I belonged to a live culture (even a smart, unqueer one) and working in a war (even just so as to get out of it fast), while a third part of me—one that I normally keep down—was very simply horrified.

Pop was back by the door with the box and 'chute, ready to make the drop.

Alice had no duties for the moment, but she'd suddenly started gathering up food cans and packing them in one bag—I couldn't figure out at first what she had in mind. Orderly housewife wouldn't be exactly my description of her occupational personality.

Then of course everything had to happen at once.

The voice said, "Make the drop!"

Alice crossed to Pop and thrust out the bag of cans toward him, writhing her lips in silent "talk" to tell him something. She had a knife in her burnt hand too.

But I didn't have time to do any lip-reading, because just then a glittering pink asterisk showed up in the darkening haze ahead—a whole half dozen straight lines spreading out from a blank central spot, as if a super-fast gigantic spider had laid in the first strands of its web.

Wind whistled as the door of the plane started to open.

I fought to center my sight on the blank central spot, which drifted toward the left.

One of the straight lines grew dazzlingly bright.

I heard Alice whisper fiercely, "Drop *these!*" and the part of my mind that couldn't be applied to gunnery instantly deduced that she'd had some last-minute inspiration about dropping a bunch of cans instead of the steel cubes.

I got the sight centered and held down the firing combo. The thought flashed to me: *it's a city you're firing at, not a plane,* and I flinched.

The dazzlingly pink line dipped down toward me.

Behind me, the sound of a struggle. Alice snarling and Pop giving a grunt.

Then all at once a scream from Alice, a big whoosh of wind, a flash way ahead (where I'd aimed), a spatter of hot metal inside the cabin, a blinding spot in the middle of the World Screen, a searing beam inches from my neck, an electric shock that lifted me from my seat and ripped at my consciousness!

When I came to (if I really ever was out—seconds later, at most) there were no more pink lines. The haze was just its disgustingly tawny evening self with black spots that were only after-images. The cabin stunk of ozone, but wind funneling through a hole in the one-time World Screen was blowing it out fast enough—Savannah had gotten in one lick, all right. And we were falling, the plane was swinging down like a crippled bird—I could feel it and there was no use kidding myself.

But staring at the control panel wouldn't keep us from crashing if that was in the cards. I looked around and there were Pop and Alice glaring at each other across the closing door. He looked mean. She looked agonized and was pressing her burnt hand into her side with her elbow as if he'd stamped on the hand, maybe. I didn't see any blood though. I didn't see the box and 'chute either, though I did see Alice's bag of groceries. I guessed Pop had made the drop.

Now, it occurred to me, was a bully time for Voice Two to melt the plane—if he hadn't already tried. My first thought had been that the spatter of hot metal had come from the Savannah craft spitting us, but there was no way to be sure.

I looked around at the viewport in time to see rocks and stunted trees jump out of the haze. *Good old Ray,* I thought, *always in at the death.* But just then the plane took a sickening bounce, as if its antigravity had only started to operate within yards of the ground. Another lurching fall and another bounce, less violent. A couple of repetitions of that, each one a little gentler, and then we were sort of bumping along on an even keel with the rocks and such sliding past fast about a hundred feet below, I judged. We'd been spoiled for altitude work, it seemed, but we could still cripple along in some sort of low-power repulsion field.

I looked at the North America screen and the buttons, wondering if I should start us back west again or leave us set on Atla-Hi and see what the hell happened—at the moment I hardly cared what else Savannah did to us. I needn't of wasted the mental energy. The decision was made for me. As I watched, the Atla-Hi button jumped up by itself and the button for the cracking plant went down and there was some extra bumping as we swung around.

Also, the violet patch of Atla-Hi went real dim and the button for it no longer had a violet nimbus. The Los Alamos blue went dull too. The cracking-plant dot glowed a brighter green—that was all.

All except for one thing. As the violet dimmed I thought I heard Voice One very faintly (not as if speaking directly but as if the screen had heard and remembered—not a voice but the fluorescent ghost of one): "Thank you and good luck!"

CHAPTER VI

Many a man has dated his ruin from some murder or other that perhaps he thought little of at the time.

—Thomas de Quincey

"AND a long merry siege to you, sir, and roast rat for Christmas!" I responded, very out loud and rather to my surprise.

"War! How I hate war!"—that was what Pop exploded with. He didn't exactly dance in senile rage—he was still keeping too sharp a watch on Alice—but his voice sounded that way.

"Damn you, Pop!" Alice contributed. "And you too, Ray! We might have pulled something, but you had to go obedience-happy." Then her anger got the better of her grammar, or maybe Pop and me was corrupting it. "Damn the both of you!" she finished.

It didn't make much sense, any of it. We were just cutting loose, I guess, after being scared to say anything for the last half hour.

I said to Alice, "I don't know what you could have pulled, except the chain on us." To Pop I remarked, "You may hate war, but you sure helped that one along. Those grenades you dropped will probably take care of a few hundred Savannans."

"That's what you always say about me, isn't it?" he snapped back. "But I don't suppose I should expect any kinder interpretation of my motives." To Alice he said, "I'm sorry I had to slap your burnt fingers, sister, but you can't say I didn't warn you about my low-down tactics." Then to me again: "I *do* hate war, Ray. It's just murder on a bigger scale, though some of the boys give me an argument there."

"Then why don't you go preach against war in Atla-Hi and Savannah?" Alice demanded, still very hot but not quite so bitter.

"Yeah, Pop, how about it?" I seconded.

"Maybe I should," he said, thoughtful all at once. "They sure need it." Then he grinned. "Hey, how'd this sound: HEAR THE WORLD-FAMOUS MURDERER POP TRUMBULL TALK AGAINST WAR. WEAR YOUR STEEL THROAT PROTECTORS. Pretty good, hey?"

We all laughed at that, grudgingly at first, then with a touch of wholeheartedness. I think we all recognized that things weren't going to be very cheerful from here on in and we'd better not turn up our noses at the feeblest fun.

"I guess I didn't have anything very bright in mind," Alice admitted to me, while to Pop she said, "All right, I forgive you for the present."

"Don't!" Pop said with a shudder. "I hate to think of what happened to the last bugger made the mistake of forgiving me."

We looked around and took stock of our resources. It was time we did. It was getting dark fast, although we were chasing the sun, and there weren't any cabin lights coming on and we sure didn't know of any way of getting any.

We wadded a couple of satchels into the hole in the World Screen without trying to probe it. After a while it got warmer again in the cabin and the air a little less dusty. Presently it started to get too smoky from the cigarettes we were burning, but that came later.

We screwed off the walls the few storage bags we hadn't inspected. They didn't contain nothing of consequence, not even a flashlight.

I had one last go at the buttons, though there weren't any left with nimbuses on them—the darker it got, the clearer that was. Even the Atla-Hi button wouldn't push now that it had lost its violet halo. I tried the gunnery patterns, figuring to put in a little time taking pot shots at any mountains that turned up, but the buttons that had been responding so well a few minutes ago refused to budge. Alice suggested different patterns, but none of them worked. That console was really locked—maybe the shot from Savannah was partly responsible, though Atla-Hi remote-locking things was explanation enough.

"The buggers!" I said. "They didn't have to tie us up *this* tight. Going east we at least had a choice—forward or back. Now we got none."

"Maybe we're just as well off," Pop said. "If Atla-Hi had been able to do anything more for us—that is, if they hadn't been sieged in, I mean—they'd sure as anything have pulled us in. Pull the plane in, I mean, and picked us out of it—with a big pair of tweezers, likely as not. And contrary to your flattering opinion of my preaching (which by the way none of the religious boys in my outfit share—they call me 'that misguided old atheist'), I don't think none of us would go over big at Atla-Hi."

We had to agree with him there. I couldn't imagine Pop or Alice or even me cutting much of a figure (even if we weren't murder-pariahs) with the pack of geniuses that seemed to make up the Atla-Alamos crowd. The Double-A Republics, to give them a name, might have their small-brain types, but somehow I didn't think so. There must be more than one Edison-Einstein, it seemed to me, back of antigravity and all the wonders in this plane and the other things we'd gotten hints of. Also, Grayl had seemed bred for brains as well as size, even if us small mammals had cooked his goose. And none of the modern "countries" had more than a few thousand population yet, I was pretty sure, and that hardly left room for a dumbbell class. Finally, too, I got hold of a memory I'd been reaching for the last hour—how when I was a kid I'd read about some scientists who learned to talk Mandarin just for kicks. I told Alice and Pop.

"And if *that's* the average Atla-Alamoser's idea of mental recreation," I said, "well, you can see what I mean."

"I'll grant you they got a monopoly of brains," Pop agreed. "Not sense, though," he added doggedly.

"Intellectual snobs," was Alice's comment. "I know the type and I detest it." ("You *are* sort of intellectual, aren't you?" Pop told her, which fortunately didn't start a riot.)

Still, I guess all three of us found it fun to chew over a bit the new slant we'd gotten on two (in a way, three) of the great "countries" of the modern world. (And as long as we thought of it as fun, we didn't have to admit the envy and wistfulness that was behind our wisecracks.)

I said, "We've always figured in a general way that Alamos was the remains of a community of scientists and technicians. Now we know the same's true of the Atla-Hi group. They're the Brookhaven survivors."

"Manhattan Project, don't you mean?" Alice corrected.

"Nope, that was in Colorado Springs," Pop said with finality.

I also pointed out that a community of scientists would educate for technical intelligence, maybe breed for it too. And being a group picked for high I. Q. to begin with, they might make startlingly fast progress. You could easily imagine such folk, unimpeded by the boobs, creating a wonder world in a couple of generations.

"They got their troubles though," Pop reminded me and that led us to speculating about the war we'd dipped into. Savannah Fortress, we knew, was supposed to be based on some big atomic plants on the river down that way, but its culture seemed to have a fiercer ingredient than Atla-Alamos. Before we knew it we were musing almost romantically about the plight of Atla-Hi, beseiged by superior and (it was easy to suppose) barbaric forces, and maybe distant Los Alamos in a similar predicament—Alice reminded me how the voice had asked if they were still dying out there. For a moment I found myself fiercely proud that I had been able to strike a blow against evil aggressors. At once, of course, then, the revulsion came.

"This is a hell of a way," I said, "for three so-called realists to be mooning about things."

"Yes, especially when your heroes kicked us out," Alice agreed.

Pop chuckled. "Yep," he said, "they even took Ray's artillery away from him."

"You're wrong there, Pop," I said, sitting up. "I still got one of the grenades—the one the pilot had in his fist." To tell the truth I'd forgotten all about it and it bothered me a little now to feel it snugged up in my pocket against my hip bone where the skin is thin.

"You believe what that old Dutchman said about the steel cubes being atomic grenades?" Pop asked me.

"I don't know," I said, "He sure didn't sound enthusiastic about telling us the truth about anything. But for that matter he sounded mean enough to tell the truth figuring we'd think it was a lie. Maybe this *is* some sort of baby A-bomb with a fuse timed like a grenade." I got it out and hefted it. "How about I press the button and drop it out the door? Then we'll know." I really felt like doing it—restless, I guess.

"Don't be a fool, Ray," Alice said.

"Don't tense up, I won't," I told her. At the same time I made myself the little promise that if I ever got to feeling restless, that is, restless and *bad*, I'd just go ahead and punch the button and see what happened—sort of leave my future up to the gods of the Deathlands, you might say.

"What makes you so sure it's a weapon?" Pop asked.

"What else would it be," I asked him, "that they'd be so hot on getting them in the middle of a war?"

"I don't know for sure," Pop said. "I've made a guess, but I don't want to tell it now. What I'm getting at, Ray, is that your first thought about anything you find—in the world outside or in your own mind—is that it's a weapon."

"Anything worthwhile in your mind is a weapon!" Alice interjected with surprising intensity.

"You see?" Pop said. "That's what I mean about the both of you. That sort of thinking's been going on a long time. Cave man picks up a rock and right away asks himself, 'Who can I brain with this?' Doesn't occur to him for several hundred thousand years to use it to start building a hospital."

"You know, Pop," I said, carefully tucking the cube back in my pocket, "you *are* sort of preachy at times."

"Guess I am," he said. "How about some grub?"

It was a good idea. Another few minutes and we wouldn't have been able to see to eat, though with the cans shaped to tell their contents I guess we'd have managed. It was a funny circumstance that in this wonder plane we didn't even know how to turn on the light—and a good measure of our general helplessness.

We had our little feed and lit up again and settled ourselves. I judged it would be an overnight trip, at least to the cracking plant—we weren't making anything like the speed we had been going east. Pop was sitting in back again and Alice and I lay half hitched around on the kneeling seats, which allowed us to watch each other. Pretty soon it got so dark we couldn't see anything of each other but the glowing tips of the cigarettes and a bit of face around the mouth when the person took a deep drag. They were a good idea, those cigarettes—kept us from having ideas about the other person starting to creep around with a knife in his hand.

The North America screen still glowed dimly and we could watch our green dot trying to make progress. The viewport was dead black at first, then there came the faintest sort of bronze blotch that very slowly shifted forward and down. The Old Moon, of course, going west ahead of us.

After a while I realized what it was like—an old Pullman car (I'd traveled in one once as a kid) or especially the smoker of an old Pullman, very late at night. Our crippled antigravity, working on the irregularities of the ground as they came along below, made the ride rhythmically bumpy, you see. I remembered how lonely and strange that old sleeping car had seemed to me as a kid. This felt the same. I kept waiting for a hoot or a whistle. It was the sort of loneliness that settles in your bones and keeps working at you.

"I recall the first man I ever killed—" Pop started to reminisce softly.

"Shut up!" Alice told him. "Don't you ever talk about anything but murder, Pop?"

"Guess not," he said. "After all, it's the only really interesting topic there is. Do you know of another?"

It was silent in the cabin for a long time after that. Then Alice said, "It was the afternoon before my twelfth birthday when they came into the kitchen and killed my father. He'd been wise, in a way, and had us living at a spot where the bombs didn't touch us or the worst fallout. But he hadn't counted on the local werewolf gang. He'd just been slicing some bread—homemade from our own wheat (Dad was great on back to nature and all)—but he laid down the knife.

"Dad couldn't see any object or idea as a weapon, you see—that was his great weakness. Dad couldn't even see weapons as weapons. Dad had a philosophy of cooperation, that was his name for it, that he was going to explain to people. Sometimes I think he was glad of the Last War, because he believed it would give him his chance.

"But the werewolves weren't interested in philosophy and although their knives weren't as sharp as Dad's they didn't lay them down. Afterwards they had themselves a meal, with me for dessert. I remember one of them used a slice of bread to sop up blood like gravy. And another washed his hands and face in the cold coffee . . ."

She didn't say anything else for a bit. Pop said softly, "That was the afternoon; wasn't it, that the fallen angels . . ." and then just said, "My big mouth."

"You were going to say 'the afternoon they killed God?'" Alice asked him. "You're right, it was. They killed God in the kitchen that afternoon. That's how I know he's dead. Afterwards they would have killed me too, eventually, except—"

Again she broke off, this time to say, "Pop, do you suppose I can have been thinking about myself as the Daughter of God all these years? That that's why everything seems so intense?"

"I don't know," Pop said. "The religious boys say we're all children of God. I don't put much stock in it—or else God sure has some lousy children. Go on with your story."

"Well, they would have killed me too, except the leader took a fancy to me and got the idea of training me up for a Weregirl or She-wolf Deb or whatever they called it.

"That was my first experience of ideas as weapons. He got an idea about me and I used it to kill him. I had to wait three months for my opportunity. I got him so lazy he let me shave him. He bled to death the same way as Dad."

"Hum," Pop commented after a bit, "that was a chiller, all right. I got to remember to tell it to Bill—it was somebody killing his mother that got *him* started. Alice, you had about as good a justification for your first murder as any I remember hearing."

"Yet," Alice said after another pause, with just a trace of the old sarcasm creeping back into her voice, "I don't suppose you think I was right to do it?"

"Right? Wrong? Who knows?" Pop said almost blusteringly. "Sure you were justified in a whole pack of ways. Anybody'd sympathize with you. A man often has fine justification for the first murder he commits. But as you must know, it's not that the first murder's always so bad in itself as that it's apt to start you on a killing spree. Your sense of values gets shifted a tiny bit and never shifts back. But you know all that and who am I to tell you anything, anyway? I've killed men because I didn't like the way they spit. And may very well do it again if I don't keep watching myself and my mind ventilated."

"Well, Pop," Alice said, "I didn't always have such dandy justification for my killings. Last one was a moony old physicist—he fixed me the Geiger counter I carry. A silly old geek—I don't know how he survived so long. Maybe an exile or a runaway. You know, I often attach myself to the elderly do-gooder type like my father was. Or like you, Pop."

Pop nodded. "It's good to know yourself," he said.

There was a third pause and then, although I hadn't exactly been intending to, I said, "Alice had justification for her first murder, personal justification that an ape would understand. I had no personal justification at all for mine, yet I killed about a million people at a modest estimate. You see, I was the boss of the crew that took care of the hydrogen missile ticketed for Moscow, and when the ticket was finally taken up I was the one to punch it. My finger on the firing button, I mean."

I went on, "Yeah, Pop, I was one of the button-pushers. There were really quite a few of us, of course—that's why I get such a laugh out of stories about being or rubbing out the *one* guy who pushed all the buttons."

"That so?" Pop said with only mild-sounding interest. "In that case you ought to know—"

We didn't get to hear right then who I ought to know because I had a fit of coughing and we realized the cigarette smoke was getting just too thick. Pop fixed the door so it was open a crack and after a while the atmosphere got reasonably okay though we had to put up with a low lonely whistling sound.

"Yeah," I continued, "I was the boss of the missile crew and I wore a very handsome uniform with impressive insignia—not the bully old stripes I got on my chest now—and I was very young and handsome myself. We were all very young in that line of service, though a few of the men under me were a little older. Young and dedicated. I remember feeling a very deep and grim—and *clean*—responsibility. But I wonder sometimes just how deep it went or how clean it really was.

"I had an uncle flew in the war they fought to lick fascism, bombadier on a Flying Fortress or something, and once when he got drunk he told me how some days it didn't bother him at all to drop the eggs on Germany; the buildings and people down there seemed just like toys that a kid sets up to kick over, and the whole business about as naive fun as poking an anthill.

"*I* didn't even have to fly over at seven miles what I was going to be aiming at. Only I remember sometimes getting out a map and looking at a certain large dot on it and smiling a little and softly saying, 'Pow!'—and then giving a little conventional shudder and folding up the map quick.

"Naturally we told ourselves we'd never have to do it, fire the thing, I mean, we joked about how after twenty years or so we'd all be given jobs as museum attendants of this same bomb, deactivated at last. But naturally it didn't work out that way. There came the day when our side of the world got hit and the orders started cascading down from Defense Coordinator Bigelow—"

"Bigelow?" Pop interrupted. "Not Joe Bigelow?"

"Joseph A., I believe," I told him, a little annoyed.

"Why he's my boy then, the one I was telling you about—the skinny runt had this horn-handle! Can you beat that?" Pop sounded startlingly happy. "Him and you'll have a lot to talk about when you get together."

I wasn't so sure of that myself, in fact my first reaction was that the opposite would be true. To be honest I was for the first moment more than a little annoyed at Pop interrupting my story of my Big Grief—for it was that to me, make no mistake. Here my story had finally been teased out of me, against all expectation, after decades of repression and in spite of dozens of assorted psychological blocks— and here was Pop interrupting it for the sake of a lot of trivial organizational gossip about Joes and Bills and Georges we'd never heard of and what they'd say or think!

But then all of a sudden I realized that I didn't really care, that it didn't feel like a Big Grief any more, that just starting to tell about it after hearing Pop and Alice tell their stories had purged it of that unnecessary weight of feeling that had made it a millstone around my neck. It seemed to me now that I could look down at Ray Baker from a considerable height (but not an angelic or contemptuously superior height) and ask myself not why he had grieved so much—that was understandable and even desirable—but why he had grieved so *uselessly* in such a stuffy little private hell.

And it *would* be interesting to find out how Joseph A. Bigelow had felt.

"How does it feel, Ray, to kill a million people?"

I realized that Alice had asked me the question several seconds back and it was hanging in the air.

"That's just what I've been trying to tell you," I told her and started to explain it all over again—the words poured out of me now. I won't put them down here—it would take too long—but they were honest words as far as I knew and they eased me.

I couldn't get over it: here were us three murderers feeling a trust and understanding and sharing a communion that I wouldn't have believed possible between *any* two or three people in the Age of the Deaders—or in *any* age, to tell the truth. It was against everything I knew of Deathland psychology, but it was happening just the same. Oh, our strange isolation had something to do with it, I knew, and that Pullman-car memory hypnotizing my mind, and our reactions to the voices and violence of Atla-Alamos, but in spite of all that I ranked it as a wonder. I felt an inward freedom and easiness that I never would have believed possible. Pop's little disorganized organization had really got hold of something, I couldn't deny it.

Three treacherous killers talking from the bottoms of their hearts and believing each other!—for it never occurred to me to doubt that Pop and Alice were feeling exactly like I was. In fact, we were all so sure of it that we didn't even mention our communion to each other. Perhaps we were a little afraid we would rub off the bloom. We just enjoyed it.

We must have talked about a thousand things that night and smoked a couple of hundred cigarettes. After a while we started taking little catnaps—we'd gotten too much off our chests and come to feel too tranquil for even our excitement to keep us awake. I remember the first time I dozed waking up with a cold start and grabbing for Mother—and then hearing Pop and Alice gabbing in the dark, and remembering what had happened, and relaxing again with a smile.

Of all things, Pop was saying, "Yep, I imagine Ray must be good to make love to, murderers almost always are, they got the fire.

It reminds me of what a guy named Fred told me, one of our boys . . ."

Mostly we took turns going to sleep, though I think there were times when all three of us were snoozing. About the fifth time I woke up, after some tighter shut-eye, the orange soup was back again outside and Alice was snoring gently in the next seat and Pop was up and had one of his knives out.

He was looking at his reflection in the viewport. His face gleamed. He was rubbing butter into it.

"Another day, another pack of troubles," he said cheerfully.

The tone of his remark jangled my nerves, as that tone generally does early in the morning. I squeezed my eyes. "Where are we?" I asked.

He poked his elbow toward the North America screen. The two green dots were almost one.

"My God, we're practically there," Alice said for me. She'd waked fast, Deathlands style.

"I know," Pop said, concentrating on what he was doing, "but I aim to be shaved before they commence landing maneuvers."

"You think automatic will land us?" Alice asked. "What if we just start circling around?"

"We can figure out what to do when it happens," Pop said, whittling away at his chin. "Until then, I'm not interested. There's still a couple of bottles of coffee in the sack. I've had mine."

I didn't join in this chit-chat because the green dots and Alice's first remark had reminded me of a lot deeper reason for my jangled nerves than Pop's cheerfulness. Night was gone, with its shielding cloak and its feeling of being able to talk forever, and the naked day was here, with its demands for action. It is not so difficult to change your whole view of life when you are flying, or even bumping along above the ground with friends who understand, but soon, I knew, I'd be down in the dust with something I never wanted to see again.

"Coffee, Ray?"

"Yeah, I guess so." I took the bottle from Alice and wondered whether my face looked as glum as hers.

"They shouldn't salt butter," Pop asserted. "It makes it lousy for shaving."

"It was the *best* butter," Alice said.

"Yeah," I said. "The Dormouse, when they buttered the watch."

It may be true that feeble humor is better than none. I don't know.

"What are you two yakking about?" Pop demanded.

"A book we both read," I told him.

"Either of you writers?" Pop asked with sudden interest. "Some of the boys think we should have a book about us. I say it's too soon, but they say we might all die off or something. Whoa, Jenny! Easy does it. Gently, please!"

That last remark was by way of recognizing that the plane had started an authoritative turn to the left. I got a sick and cold feeling. This was it.

Pop sheathed his knife and gave his face a final rub. Alice belted on her satchel. I reached for my knapsack, but I was staring through the viewport, dead ahead.

The haze lightened faintly, three times. I remembered the St. Elmo's fire that had flamed from the cracking plant.

"Pop," I said—almost whined, to be truthful, "why'd the bugger ever have to land here in the first place? He was rushing stuff they needed bad at Atla-Hi—why'd he have to break his trip?"

"That's easy," Pop said. "He was being a bad boy. At least that's my theory. He was supposed to go straight to Atla-Hi, but there was somebody he wanted to check up on first. He stopped here to see his girlfriend. Yep, his girlfriend. She tried to warn him off—that's my explanation of the juice that flared out of the cracking plant and interfered with his landing, though I'm sure she didn't intend the last. By the way, whatever she turned on to give him the warning must still be turned on. But Grayl came on down in spite of it."

Before I could assimilate that, the seven deformed gas tanks materialized in the haze. We got the freeway in our sights and steadied and slowed and kept slowing. The plane didn't graze the cracking plant this time, though I'd have sworn it was going to hit it head on. When I saw we *weren't* going to hit it, I wanted to shut my eyes, but I couldn't.

The stain was black now and the Pilot's body was thicker than I remembered—bloated. But that wouldn't last long. Three or four vultures were working on it.

CHAPTER VII

Here now in his triumph where all things falter,
Stretched out on the spoils that his own hand spread,
As a god self-slain on his own strange altar,
Death lies dead.

—A Forsaken Garden,
by Charles Swinburne

Pop was first down. Between us we helped Alice. Before joining them I took a last look at the control panel. The cracking plant button was up again and there was a blue nimbus on another button. For Las Alamos, I supposed. I was tempted to push it and get away solo, but then I thought, *nope, there's nothing for me at the other end and the loneliness will be worse than what I got to face here.* I climbed out.

I didn't look at the body, although we were practically on top of it. I saw a little patch of silver off to one side and remembered the gun that had melted. The vultures had waddled off but only a few yards. "We could kill them," Alice said to Pop.

"Why?" he responded. "Didn't some Hindus use them to take care of dead bodies? Not a bad idea, either."

"Parsees," Alice amplified.

"Yep, Parsees, that's what I meant. Give you a nice clean skeleton in a matter of days."

Pop was leading us past the body toward the cracking plant. I heard the flies buzzing loudly. I felt terrible. I wanted to be dead myself. Just walking along after Pop was an awful effort.

"His girl was running a hidden observation tower here," Pop was saying now. "Weather and all that, I suppose. Or maybe setting up a robot station of some kind. I couldn't tell you about her before, because you were both in a mood to try to rub out anybody remotely connected with the Pilot. In fact, I did my best to lead you astray, letting you think I'd been the one to scream and all. Even now, to be honest about it, I don't know if I'm doing the right thing telling and showing you all this, but a man's got to take some risks whatever he does."

"Say Pop," I said dully, "isn't she apt to take a shot at us or something?" Not that I'd have minded on my own account. "Or are you and her that good friends?"

"Nope, Ray," he said, "she doesn't even know me. But I don't think she's in a position to do any shooting. You'll see why. Hey, she hasn't even shut the door. That's bad."

He seemed to be referring to a kind of manhole cover standing on its edge just inside the open-walled first story of the cracking plant. He knelt and looked down the hole the cover was designed to close off.

"Well, at least she didn't collapse at the bottom of the shaft," he said. "Come on, let's see what happened." And he climbed into the shaft.

We followed him like zombies. At least that's how I felt. The shaft was about twenty feet deep. There were foot- and hand-holds. It got stuffy right away, and warmer, in spite of the shaft being open at the top.

At the bottom there was a short horizontal passage. We had to duck to get through it. When we could straighten up we were in a large and luxurious bomb-resistant dugout, to give it a name. And it was stuffier and hotter than ever.

There was a lot of scientific equipment around and several small control panels reminding me of the one in the back of the plane. Some of them, I supposed, connected with instruments, weather and otherwise, hidden up in the skeletal structure of the cracking plant.

And there were signs of occupancy, a young woman's occupancy—clothes scattered around in a frivolous way, and some small objects of art, and a slightly more than life-size head in clay that I guessed the occupant must have been sculpting. I didn't give that last more than the most fleeting look, strictly unintentional to begin with, because although it wasn't finished I could tell whose head it was supposed to be—the Pilot's.

The whole place was finished in dull silver like the cabin of the plane, and likewise it instantly struck me as having a living personality, partly the Pilot's and partly someone else's—the personality of a marriage. Which wasn't a bit nice, because the whole place smelt of death.

But to tell the truth I didn't give the place more than the quickest look-over, because my attention was riveted almost at once on a long wide couch with the covers kicked off it and on the body there.

The woman was about six feet tall and built like a goddess. Her hair was blonde and her skin tanned. She was lying on her stomach and she was naked.

She didn't come anywhere near my libido, though. She looked sick to death. Her face, twisted towards us, was hollow-cheeked and flushed. Her eyes, closed, were sunken and dark-circled. She was breathing shallowly and rapidly through her open mouth, gasping now and then.

I got the crazy impression that all the heat in the place was coming from her body, radiating from her fever.

And the whole place stunk of death. Honestly it seemed to me that this dugout was Death's underground temple, the bed Death's altar, and the woman Death's sacrifice. (Had I unconsciously come to worship Death as a god in the Deathlands? I don't really know. There it gets too deep for me.)

No, she didn't come within a million miles of my libido, but there was another part of me that she was eating at …

If guilt's a luxury, then I'm a plutocrat.

. . . eating at until I was an empty shell, until I had no props left, until I wanted to die then and there, until I figured I had to die . . .

There was a faint sharp hiss right at my elbow. I looked and found that, unbeknownst to myself, I'd taken the steel cube out of my pocket and holding it snuggled between my first and second fingers I'd punched the button with my thumb just as I'd promised myself I would if I got to really feeling bad.

It goes to show you that you should never give your mind any kind of instructions even half in fun, unless you're prepared to have them carried out whether you approve later or not.

Pop saw what I'd done and looked at me strangely. "So you had to die after all, Ray," he said softly. "Most of us find out we have to, one way or another."

We waited. Nothing happened. I noticed a very faint milky cloud a few inches across hanging in the air by the cube.

Thinking right away of poison gas, I jerked away a little, dispersing the cloud.

"What's that?" I demanded of no one in particular.

"I'd say," said Pop, "that that's something that squirted out of a tiny hole in the side of the cube opposite the button. A hole so nearly microscopic you wouldn't see it unless you looked for it hard. Ray, I don't think you're going to get your baby A-blast, and what's more I'm afraid you've wasted something that's damn valuable. But don't let it worry you. Before I dropped those cubes for Atla-Hi I snagged one."

And darn if he didn't pull the brother of my cube out of his pocket.

"Alice," he said, "'I noticed a half pint of whiskey in your satchel when we got the salve. Would you put some on a rag and hand it to me."

Alice looked at him like he was nuts, but while her eyes were looking her pliers and her gloved hand were doing what he told her.

Pop took the rag and swabbed a spot on the sick woman's nearest buttock and jammed the cube against the spot and pushed the button.

"It's a jet hypodermic, folks," he said.

He took the cube away and there was the welt to substantiate his statement.

"Hope we got to her in time," he said. "The plague is tough. Now I guess there's nothing for us to do but wait, maybe for quite a while."

I felt shaken beyond all recognition.

"Pop, you old caveman detective!" I burst out. "When did you get that idea for a steel hospital?" Don't think I was feeling anywhere near that gay. It was reaction, close to hysterical.

Pop was taken aback, but then he grinned. "I had a couple of clues that you and Alice didn't," he said. "I knew there was a very sick woman involved. And I had that bout with Los Alamos fever I told you. They've had a lot of trouble with it, I believe—some say its spores come from outside the world with the cosmic dust—and now it seems to have been carried to Atla-Hi. Let's hope they've found the answer this time. Alice, maybe we'd better start getting some water into this gal."

After a while we sat down and fitted the facts together more orderly. Pop did the fitting mostly. Alamos researchers must have been working for years on the plague as it ravaged intermittently, maybe with mutations and ET tricks to make the job harder. Very recently they'd found a promising treatment (cure, we hoped) and prepared it for rush shipment to Atla-Hi, where the plague was raging too and they were sieged in by Savannah as well. Grayl was picked to fly the serum, or drug, or whatever it was. But he knew or guessed that this lone woman observer (because she'd fallen out of radio communication or something) had come down with the plague too and he decided to land some serum for her, probably without authorization.

"How do we know she's his girlfriend?" I asked.

"Or wife," Pop said tolerantly. "Why, there was that bag of woman's stuff he was carrying, frilly things like a man would bring for a woman. Who else'd he be apt to make a special stop for?

"Another thing," Pop said. "He must have been using jets to hurry his trip. We heard them, you know."

That seemed about as close a reconstruction of events as we could get. Strictly hypothetical, of course. Deathlanders trying to figure out what goes on inside a "country" like Atla-Alamos and *why* are sort of like foxes trying to understand world politics, or wolves the Gothic migrations. Of course we're all human beings, but that doesn't mean as much as it sounds.

Then Pop told us how he'd happened to be on the scene. He'd been doing a "tour of duty," as he called it, when he spotted this woman's observatory and decided to hang around anonymously and watch over her for a few days and maybe help protect her from some dangerous characters that he knew were in the neighborhood.

"Pop, that sounds like a lousy idea to me," I objected. "Risky, I mean. Spying on another person, watching them without their knowing, would be the surest way to stir up in me the idea of murdering them. Safest thing for me to do in that situation would be to turn around and run."

"*You* probably should," he agreed. "For now, anyway. It's all a matter of knowing your own strength and stage of growth. Me, it helps to give myself these little jobs. And the essence of 'em is that the other person shouldn't know I'm helping."

It sounded like knighthood and pilgrimage and the Boy Scouts all over again—for murderers. Well, why not?

Pop had seen this woman come out of the manhole a couple of times and look around and then go back down and he'd got the impression she was sick and troubled. He'd even guessed she might be coming down with Alamos fever. He'd seen us arrive, of course, and that had bothered him. Then when the plane landed she'd come up again, acting out of her head, but when she'd seen the Pilot and us going for him she'd given that scream and collapsed at the top of the shaft. He'd figured the only thing he could do for her was keep us occupied. Besides, now that he knew for sure we were murderers he'd started to burn with the desire to talk to us and maybe help us quit killing if we seemed to want to. It was only much later, in the middle of our trip, that he began to suspect that the steel cubes were jet hypodermics.

While Pop had been telling us all his, we hadn't been watching the woman so closely. Now Alice called our attention to her. Her skin was covered with fine beads of perspiration, like diamonds.

"That's a good sign," Pop said, and Alice started to wipe her off. While she was doing that the woman came to in a groggy sort of way and Pop fed her some thin soup and in the middle of his doing it she dropped off to sleep.

Alice said, "Any other time I would be wild to kill another woman that beautiful. But she has been so close to death that I would feel I was robbing another murderer. I suppose there is more behind the change in my feelings than that, though."

"Yeah, a little, I suppose," Pop said.

I didn't have anything to say about my own feelings. Certainly not out loud. I knew that they had changed and that they were still changing. It was complicated.

After a while it occurred to me and Alice to worry whether we mightn't catch this woman's sickness. It would serve us right, of course, but plague is plague. But Pop reassured us. "Actually I snagged three cubes," he said. "That should take care of you two. I figure I'm immune."

Time wore on. Pop dragged out the harmonica, as I'd been afraid he would, but his playing wasn't too bad. "Tenting Tonight," "When Johnnie Comes Marching Home," and such. We had a meal.

The Pilot's woman woke up again, in her full mind this time or something like it. We were clustered around the bed, smiling a little I suppose and looking inquiring. Being even assistant nurses makes you all concerned about the patient's health and state of mind.

Pop helped her sit up a little. She looked around. She saw me and Alice. Recognition came into her eyes. She drew away from us with a look of loathing. She didn't say a word, but the look stayed.

Pop drew me aside and whispered, "I think it would be a nice gesture if you and Alice took a blanket and went up and sewed him into it. I noticed a big needle and some thread in her satchel." He looked me in the eye and added, "You can't expect this woman to feel any other way toward you, you know. Now or ever."

He was right, of course. I gave Alice the high sign and we got out.

No point in dwelling on the next scene. Alice and me sewed up in a blanket a big guy who'd been dead a day and worked over by vultures. That's all.

About the time we'd finished, Pop came up.

"She chased me out," he explained. "She's getting dressed. When I told her about the plane, she said she was going back to Los Alamos. She's not fit to travel, of course, but she's giving herself injections. It's none of our business. Incidentally, she wants to take the body back with her. I told her how we'd dropped the serum and how you and Alice had helped and she listened."

The Pilot's woman wasn't long after Pop. She must have had trouble getting up the shaft, she had a little trouble even walking straight, but she held her head high. She was wearing a dull silver tunic and sandals and cloak. As she passed me and Alice I could see the look of loathing come back into her eyes, and her chin went a little higher. I thought, why shouldn't she want us dead? Right now she probably wants to be dead herself.

Pop nodded to us and we hoisted up the body and followed her. It was almost too heavy a load even for the three of us.

As she reached the plane a silver ladder telescoped down to her from below the door. I thought, *the Pilot must have had it keyed to her some way, so it would let down for her but nobody else. A very lovely gesture.*

The ladder went up after her and we managed to lift the body above our heads, our arms straight, and we walked it through the door of the plane that way, she receiving it.

The door closed and we stood back and the plane took off into the orange haze, us watching it until it was swallowed.

Pop said, "Right now, I imagine you two feel pretty good in a screwed-up sort of way. I know I do. But take it from me, it won't last. A day or two and we're going to start feeling another way, the *old* way, if we don't get busy."

I knew he was right. You don't shake Old Urge Number One anything like that easy.

"So," said Pop, "I got places I want to show you. Guys I want you to meet. And there's things to do, a lot of them. Let's get moving."

So there's my story. Alice is still with me (Urge Number Two is even harder to shake, supposing you wanted to) and we haven't killed anybody lately. (Not since the Pilot, in fact, but it doesn't do to boast.) We're making a stab (my language!) at doing the sort of work Pop does in the Deathlands. It's tough but interesting. I still carry a knife, but I've given Mother to Pop. He has it strapped to him alongside Alice's screw-in blade.

Atla-Hi and Alamos still seem to be in existence, so I guess the serum worked for them generally as it did for the Pilot's Woman; they haven't sent us any medals, but they haven't sent a hangman's squad after us either—which is more than fair, you'll admit. But Savannah, turned back from Atla-Hi, is still going strong: there's a rumor they have an army at the gates of Ouachita right now. We tell Pop he'd better start preaching fast—it's one of our standard jokes.

There's also a rumor that a certain fellowship of Deathlanders is doing surprisingly well, a rumor that there's a new America growing in the Deathlands—an America that never need kill again. But don't put too much stock in it. Not *too* much.

THE END

A CATALOG OF SELECTED
DOVER BOOKS
IN ALL FIELDS OF INTEREST

A CATALOG OF SELECTED DOVER BOOKS IN ALL FIELDS OF INTEREST

100 BEST-LOVED POEMS, Edited by Philip Smith. "The Passionate Shepherd to His Love," "Shall I compare thee to a summer's day?" "Death, be not proud," "The Raven," "The Road Not Taken," plus works by Blake, Wordsworth, Byron, Shelley, Keats, many others. 96pp. $5\frac{3}{16}$ x $8\frac{1}{4}$. 0-486-28553-7

100 SMALL HOUSES OF THE THIRTIES, Brown-Blodgett Company. Exterior photographs and floor plans for 100 charming structures. Illustrations of models accompanied by descriptions of interiors, color schemes, closet space, and other amenities. 200 illustrations. 112pp. $8\frac{3}{8}$ x 11. 0-486-44131-8

1000 TURN-OF-THE-CENTURY HOUSES: With Illustrations and Floor Plans, Herbert C. Chivers. Reproduced from a rare edition, this showcase of homes ranges from cottages and bungalows to sprawling mansions. Each house is meticulously illustrated and accompanied by complete floor plans. 256pp. $9\frac{3}{8}$ x $12\frac{1}{4}$. 0-486-45596-3

101 GREAT AMERICAN POEMS, Edited by The American Poetry & Literacy Project. Rich treasury of verse from the 19th and 20th centuries includes works by Edgar Allan Poe, Robert Frost, Walt Whitman, Langston Hughes, Emily Dickinson, T. S. Eliot, other notables. 96pp. $5\frac{3}{16}$ x $8\frac{1}{4}$. 0-486-40158-8

101 GREAT SAMURAI PRINTS, Utagawa Kuniyoshi. Kuniyoshi was a master of the warrior woodblock print — and these 18th-century illustrations represent the pinnacle of his craft. Full-color portraits of renowned Japanese samurais pulse with movement, passion, and remarkably fine detail. 112pp. $8\frac{3}{8}$ x 11. 0-486-46523-3

ABC OF BALLET, Janet Grosser. Clearly worded, abundantly illustrated little guide defines basic ballet-related terms: arabesque, battement, pas de chat, relevé, sissonne, many others. Pronunciation guide included. Excellent primer. 48pp. $4\frac{3}{16}$ x $5\frac{3}{4}$. 0-486-40871-X

ACCESSORIES OF DRESS: An Illustrated Encyclopedia, Katherine Lester and Bess Viola Oerke. Illustrations of hats, veils, wigs, cravats, shawls, shoes, gloves, and other accessories enhance an engaging commentary that reveals the humor and charm of the many-sided story of accessorized apparel. 644 figures and 59 plates. 608pp. $6\frac{1}{8}$ x $9\frac{1}{4}$. 0-486-43378-1

ADVENTURES OF HUCKLEBERRY FINN, Mark Twain. Join Huck and Jim as their boyhood adventures along the Mississippi River lead them into a world of excitement, danger, and self-discovery. Humorous narrative, lyrical descriptions of the Mississippi valley, and memorable characters. 224pp. $5\frac{3}{16}$ x $8\frac{1}{4}$. 0-486-28061-6

ALICE STARMORE'S BOOK OF FAIR ISLE KNITTING, Alice Starmore. A noted designer from the region of Scotland's Fair Isle explores the history and techniques of this distinctive, stranded-color knitting style and provides copious illustrated instructions for 14 original knitwear designs. 208pp. $8\frac{3}{8}$ x $10\frac{7}{8}$. 0-486-47218-3

Browse over 9,000 books at www.doverpublications.com

ALICE'S ADVENTURES IN WONDERLAND, Lewis Carroll. Beloved classic about a little girl lost in a topsy-turvy land and her encounters with the White Rabbit, March Hare, Mad Hatter, Cheshire Cat, and other delightfully improbable characters. 42 illustrations by Sir John Tenniel. 96pp. 5¾₆ x 8¼. 0-486-27543-4

AMERICA'S LIGHTHOUSES: An Illustrated History, Francis Ross Holland. Profusely illustrated fact-filled survey of American lighthouses since 1716. Over 200 stations — East, Gulf, and West coasts, Great Lakes, Hawaii, Alaska, Puerto Rico, the Virgin Islands, and the Mississippi and St. Lawrence Rivers. 240pp. 8 x 10¾.
0-486-25576-X

AN ENCYCLOPEDIA OF THE VIOLIN, Alberto Bachmann. Translated by Frederick H. Martens. Introduction by Eugene Ysaye. First published in 1925, this renowned reference remains unsurpassed as a source of essential information, from construction and evolution to repertoire and technique. Includes a glossary and 73 illustrations. 496pp. 6⅛ x 9¼. 0-486-46618-3

ANIMALS: 1,419 Copyright-Free Illustrations of Mammals, Birds, Fish, Insects, etc., Selected by Jim Harter. Selected for its visual impact and ease of use, this outstanding collection of wood engravings presents over 1,000 species of animals in extremely lifelike poses. Includes mammals, birds, reptiles, amphibians, fish, insects, and other invertebrates. 284pp. 9 x 12. 0-486-23766-4

THE ANNALS, Tacitus. Translated by Alfred John Church and William Jackson Brodribb. This vital chronicle of Imperial Rome, written by the era's great historian, spans A.D. 14-68 and paints incisive psychological portraits of major figures, from Tiberius to Nero. 416pp. 5¾₆ x 8¼. 0-486-45236-0

ANTIGONE, Sophocles. Filled with passionate speeches and sensitive probing of moral and philosophical issues, this powerful and often-performed Greek drama reveals the grim fate that befalls the children of Oedipus. Footnotes. 64pp. 5¾₆ x 8 ¼. 0-486-27804-2

ART DECO DECORATIVE PATTERNS IN FULL COLOR, Christian Stoll. Reprinted from a rare 1910 portfolio, 160 sensuous and exotic images depict a breathtaking array of florals, geometrics, and abstracts — all elegant in their stark simplicity. 64pp. 8⅜ x 11. 0-486-44862-2

THE ARTHUR RACKHAM TREASURY: 86 Full-Color Illustrations, Arthur Rackham. Selected and Edited by Jeff A. Menges. A stunning treasury of 86 full-page plates span the famed English artist's career, from *Rip Van Winkle* (1905) to masterworks such as *Undine, A Midsummer Night's Dream,* and *Wind in the Willows* (1939). 96pp. 8⅜ x 11.
0-486-44685-9

THE AUTHENTIC GILBERT & SULLIVAN SONGBOOK, W. S. Gilbert and A. S. Sullivan. The most comprehensive collection available, this songbook includes selections from every one of Gilbert and Sullivan's light operas. Ninety-two numbers are presented uncut and unedited, and in their original keys. 410pp. 9 x 12.
0-486-23482-7

THE AWAKENING, Kate Chopin. First published in 1899, this controversial novel of a New Orleans wife's search for love outside a stifling marriage shocked readers. Today, it remains a first-rate narrative with superb characterization. New introductory Note. 128pp. 5¾₆ x 8¼. 0-486-27786-0

BASIC DRAWING, Louis Priscilla. Beginning with perspective, this commonsense manual progresses to the figure in movement, light and shade, anatomy, drapery, composition, trees and landscape, and outdoor sketching. Black-and-white illustrations throughout. 128pp. 8⅜ x 11. 0-486-45815-6

THE BATTLES THAT CHANGED HISTORY, Fletcher Pratt. Historian profiles 16 crucial conflicts, ancient to modern, that changed the course of Western civilization. Gripping accounts of battles led by Alexander the Great, Joan of Arc, Ulysses S. Grant, other commanders. 27 maps. 352pp. 5⅜ x 8½.   0-486-41129-X

BEETHOVEN'S LETTERS, Ludwig van Beethoven. Edited by Dr. A. C. Kalischer. Features 457 letters to fellow musicians, friends, greats, patrons, and literary men. Reveals musical thoughts, quirks of personality, insights, and daily events. Includes 15 plates. 410pp. 5⅜ x 8½.   0-486-22769-3

BERNICE BOBS HER HAIR AND OTHER STORIES, F. Scott Fitzgerald. This brilliant anthology includes 6 of Fitzgerald's most popular stories: "The Diamond as Big as the Ritz," the title tale, "The Offshore Pirate," "The Ice Palace," "The Jelly Bean," and "May Day." 176pp. 5⅜ x 8½.   0-486-47049-0

BESLER'S BOOK OF FLOWERS AND PLANTS: 73 Full-Color Plates from Hortus Eystettensis, 1613, Basilius Besler. Here is a selection of magnificent plates from the *Hortus Eystettensis*, which vividly illustrated and identified the plants, flowers, and trees that thrived in the legendary German garden at Eichstätt. 80pp. 8⅜ x 11.
0-486-46005-3

THE BOOK OF KELLS, Edited by Blanche Cirker. Painstakingly reproduced from a rare facsimile edition, this volume contains full-page decorations, portraits, illustrations, plus a sampling of textual leaves with exquisite calligraphy and ornamentation. 32 full-color illustrations. 32pp. 9⅜ x 12¼.   0-486-24345-1

THE BOOK OF THE CROSSBOW: With an Additional Section on Catapults and Other Siege Engines, Ralph Payne-Gallwey. Fascinating study traces history and use of crossbow as military and sporting weapon, from Middle Ages to modern times. Also covers related weapons: balistas, catapults, Turkish bows, more. Over 240 illustrations. 400pp. 7¼ x 10¼.   0-486-28720-3

THE BUNGALOW BOOK: Floor Plans and Photos of 112 Houses, 1910, Henry L. Wilson. Here are 112 of the most popular and economic blueprints of the early 20th century — plus an illustration or photograph of each completed house. A wonderful time capsule that still offers a wealth of valuable insights. 160pp. 8⅜ x 11.
0-486-45104-6

THE CALL OF THE WILD, Jack London. A classic novel of adventure, drawn from London's own experiences as a Klondike adventurer, relating the story of a heroic dog caught in the brutal life of the Alaska Gold Rush. Note. 64pp. 5³⁄₁₆ x 8¼.
0-486-26472-6

CANDIDE, Voltaire. Edited by Francois-Marie Arouet. One of the world's great satires since its first publication in 1759. Witty, caustic skewering of romance, science, philosophy, religion, government — nearly all human ideals and institutions. 112pp. 5³⁄₁₆ x 8¼.   0-486-26689-3

CELEBRATED IN THEIR TIME: Photographic Portraits from the George Grantham Bain Collection, Edited by Amy Pastan. With an Introduction by Michael Carlebach. Remarkable portrait gallery features 112 rare images of Albert Einstein, Charlie Chaplin, the Wright Brothers, Henry Ford, and other luminaries from the worlds of politics, art, entertainment, and industry. 128pp. 8⅜ x 11.   0-486-46754-6

CHARIOTS FOR APOLLO: The NASA History of Manned Lunar Spacecraft to 1969, Courtney G. Brooks, James M. Grimwood, and Loyd S. Swenson, Jr. This illustrated history by a trio of experts is the definitive reference on the Apollo spacecraft and lunar modules. It traces the vehicles' design, development, and operation in space. More than 100 photographs and illustrations. 576pp. 6¾ x 9¼. 0-486-46756-2

Browse over 9,000 books at www.doverpublications.com

A CHRISTMAS CAROL, Charles Dickens. This engrossing tale relates Ebenezer Scrooge's ghostly journeys through Christmases past, present, and future and his ultimate transformation from a harsh and grasping old miser to a charitable and compassionate human being. 80pp. 5³⁄₁₆ x 8¼. 0-486-26865-9

COMMON SENSE, Thomas Paine. First published in January of 1776, this highly influential landmark document clearly and persuasively argued for American separation from Great Britain and paved the way for the Declaration of Independence. 64pp. 5³⁄₁₆ x 8¼. 0-486-29602-4

THE COMPLETE SHORT STORIES OF OSCAR WILDE, Oscar Wilde. Complete texts of "The Happy Prince and Other Tales," "A House of Pomegranates," "Lord Arthur Savile's Crime and Other Stories," "Poems in Prose," and "The Portrait of Mr. W. H." 208pp. 5³⁄₁₆ x 8¼. 0-486-45216-6

COMPLETE SONNETS, William Shakespeare. Over 150 exquisite poems deal with love, friendship, the tyranny of time, beauty's evanescence, death, and other themes in language of remarkable power, precision, and beauty. Glossary of archaic terms. 80pp. 5³⁄₁₆ x 8¼. 0-486-26686-9

THE COUNT OF MONTE CRISTO: Abridged Edition, Alexandre Dumas. Falsely accused of treason, Edmond Dantès is imprisoned in the bleak Chateau d'If. After a hair-raising escape, he launches an elaborate plot to extract a bitter revenge against those who betrayed him. 448pp. 5³⁄₁₆ x 8¼. 0-486-45643-9

CRAFTSMAN BUNGALOWS: Designs from the Pacific Northwest, Yoho & Merritt. This reprint of a rare catalog, showcasing the charming simplicity and cozy style of Craftsman bungalows, is filled with photos of completed homes, plus floor plans and estimated costs. An indispensable resource for architects, historians, and illustrators. 112pp. 10 x 7. 0-486-46875-5

CRAFTSMAN BUNGALOWS: 59 Homes from "The Craftsman," Edited by Gustav Stickley. Best and most attractive designs from Arts and Crafts Movement publication — 1903–1916 — includes sketches, photographs of homes, floor plans, descriptive text. 128pp. 8¼ x 11. 0-486-25829-7

CRIME AND PUNISHMENT, Fyodor Dostoyevsky. Translated by Constance Garnett. Supreme masterpiece tells the story of Raskolnikov, a student tormented by his own thoughts after he murders an old woman. Overwhelmed by guilt and terror, he confesses and goes to prison. 480pp. 5³⁄₁₆ x 8¼. 0-486-41587-2

THE DECLARATION OF INDEPENDENCE AND OTHER GREAT DOCUMENTS OF AMERICAN HISTORY: 1775-1865, Edited by John Grafton. Thirteen compelling and influential documents: Henry's "Give Me Liberty or Give Me Death," Declaration of Independence, The Constitution, Washington's First Inaugural Address, The Monroe Doctrine, The Emancipation Proclamation, Gettysburg Address, more. 64pp. 5³⁄₁₆ x 8¼. 0-486-41124-9

THE DESERT AND THE SOWN: Travels in Palestine and Syria, Gertrude Bell. "The female Lawrence of Arabia," Gertrude Bell wrote captivating, perceptive accounts of her travels in the Middle East. This intriguing narrative, accompanied by 160 photos, traces her 1905 sojourn in Lebanon, Syria, and Palestine. 368pp. 5⅜ x 8½. 0-486-46876-3

A DOLL'S HOUSE, Henrik Ibsen. Ibsen's best-known play displays his genius for realistic prose drama. An expression of women's rights, the play climaxes when the central character, Nora, rejects a smothering marriage and life in "a doll's house." 80pp. 5³⁄₁₆ x 8¼. 0-486-27062-9

Browse over 9,000 books at www.doverpublications.com

DOOMED SHIPS: Great Ocean Liner Disasters, William H. Miller, Jr. Nearly 200 photographs, many from private collections, highlight tales of some of the vessels whose pleasure cruises ended in catastrophe: the *Morro Castle, Normandie, Andrea Doria, Europa,* and many others. 128pp. 8⅞ x 11¾.　　　　0-486-45366-9

THE DORÉ BIBLE ILLUSTRATIONS, Gustave Doré. Detailed plates from the Bible: the Creation scenes, Adam and Eve, horrifying visions of the Flood, the battle sequences with their monumental crowds, depictions of the life of Jesus, 241 plates in all. 241pp. 9 x 12.　　　　0-486-23004-X

DRAWING DRAPERY FROM HEAD TO TOE, Cliff Young. Expert guidance on how to draw shirts, pants, skirts, gloves, hats, and coats on the human figure, including folds in relation to the body, pull and crush, action folds, creases, more. Over 200 drawings. 48pp. 8¼ x 11.　　　　0-486-45591-2

DUBLINERS, James Joyce. A fine and accessible introduction to the work of one of the 20th century's most influential writers, this collection features 15 tales, including a masterpiece of the short-story genre, "The Dead." 160pp. 5³⁄₁₆ x 8¼.
0-486-26870-5

EASY-TO-MAKE POP-UPS, Joan Irvine. Illustrated by Barbara Reid. Dozens of wonderful ideas for three-dimensional paper fun — from holiday greeting cards with moving parts to a pop-up menagerie. Easy-to-follow, illustrated instructions for more than 30 projects. 299 black-and-white illustrations. 96pp. 8⅞ x 11.
0-486-44622-0

EASY-TO-MAKE STORYBOOK DOLLS: A "Novel" Approach to Cloth Dollmaking, Sherralyn St. Clair. Favorite fictional characters come alive in this unique beginner's dollmaking guide. Includes patterns for Pollyanna, Dorothy from *The Wonderful Wizard of Oz,* Mary of *The Secret Garden,* plus easy-to-follow instructions, 263 black-and-white illustrations, and an 8-page color insert. 112pp. 8¼ x 11.　　0-486-47360-0

EINSTEIN'S ESSAYS IN SCIENCE, Albert Einstein. Speeches and essays in accessible, everyday language profile influential physicists such as Niels Bohr and Isaac Newton. They also explore areas of physics to which the author made major contributions. 128pp. 5 x 8.　　　　0-486-47011-3

EL DORADO: Further Adventures of the Scarlet Pimpernel, Baroness Orczy. A popular sequel to *The Scarlet Pimpernel,* this suspenseful story recounts the Pimpernel's attempts to rescue the Dauphin from imprisonment during the French Revolution. An irresistible blend of intrigue, period detail, and vibrant characterizations. 352pp. 5³⁄₁₆ x 8¼.　　　　0-486-44026-5

ELEGANT SMALL HOMES OF THE TWENTIES: 99 Designs from a Competition, Chicago Tribune. Nearly 100 designs for five- and six-room houses feature New England and Southern colonials, Normandy cottages, stately Italianate dwellings, and other fascinating snapshots of American domestic architecture of the 1920s. 112pp. 9 x 12.　　　　0-486-46910-7

THE ELEMENTS OF STYLE: The Original Edition, William Strunk, Jr. This is the book that generations of writers have relied upon for timeless advice on grammar, diction, syntax, and other essentials. In concise terms, it identifies the principal requirements of proper style and common errors. 64pp. 5⅜ x 8½.　　0-486-44798-7

THE ELUSIVE PIMPERNEL, Baroness Orczy. Robespierre's revolutionaries find their wicked schemes thwarted by the heroic Pimpernel — Sir Percival Blakeney. In this thrilling sequel, Chauvelin devises a plot to eliminate the Pimpernel and his wife. 272pp. 5³⁄₁₆ x 8¼.　　　　0-486-45464-9

Browse over 9,000 books at www.doverpublications.com

AN ENCYCLOPEDIA OF BATTLES: Accounts of Over 1,560 Battles from 1479 B.C. to the Present, David Eggenberger. Essential details of every major battle in recorded history from the first battle of Megiddo in 1479 B.C. to Grenada in 1984. List of battle maps. 99 illustrations. 544pp. 6½ x 9¼. 0-486-24913-1

ENCYCLOPEDIA OF EMBROIDERY STITCHES, INCLUDING CREWEL, Marion Nichols. Precise explanations and instructions, clearly illustrated, on how to work chain, back, cross, knotted, woven stitches, and many more — 178 in all, including Cable Outline, Whipped Satin, and Eyelet Buttonhole. Over 1400 illustrations. 219pp. 8⅜ x 11¼. 0-486-22929-7

ENTER JEEVES: 15 Early Stories, P. G. Wodehouse. Splendid collection contains first 8 stories featuring Bertie Wooster, the deliciously dim aristocrat and Jeeves, his brainy, imperturbable manservant. Also, the complete Reggie Pepper (Bertie's prototype) series. 288pp. 5⅜ x 8½. 0-486-29717-9

ERIC SLOANE'S AMERICA: Paintings in Oil, Michael Wigley. With a Foreword by Mimi Sloane. Eric Sloane's evocative oils of America's landscape and material culture shimmer with immense historical and nostalgic appeal. This original hardcover collection gathers nearly a hundred of his finest paintings, with subjects ranging from New England to the American Southwest. 128pp. 10⅝ x 9.
0-486-46525-X

ETHAN FROME, Edith Wharton. Classic story of wasted lives, set against a bleak New England background. Superbly delineated characters in a hauntingly grim tale of thwarted love. Considered by many to be Wharton's masterpiece. 96pp. 5³⁄₁₆ x 8 ¼.
0-486-26690-7

THE EVERLASTING MAN, G. K. Chesterton. Chesterton's view of Christianity — as a blend of philosophy and mythology, satisfying intellect and spirit — applies to his brilliant book, which appeals to readers' heads as well as their hearts. 288pp. 5⅜ x 8½.
0-486-46036-3

THE FIELD AND FOREST HANDY BOOK, Daniel Beard. Written by a co-founder of the Boy Scouts, this appealing guide offers illustrated instructions for building kites, birdhouses, boats, igloos, and other fun projects, plus numerous helpful tips for campers. 448pp. 5³⁄₁₆ x 8¼. 0-486-46191-2

FINDING YOUR WAY WITHOUT MAP OR COMPASS, Harold Gatty. Useful, instructive manual shows would-be explorers, hikers, bikers, scouts, sailors, and survivalists how to find their way outdoors by observing animals, weather patterns, shifting sands, and other elements of nature. 288pp. 5⅜ x 8½. 0-486-40613-X

FIRST FRENCH READER: A Beginner's Dual-Language Book, Edited and Translated by Stanley Appelbaum. This anthology introduces 50 legendary writers — Voltaire, Balzac, Baudelaire, Proust, more — through passages from *The Red and the Black, Les Misérables, Madame Bovary,* and other classics. Original French text plus English translation on facing pages. 240pp. 5⅜ x 8½. 0-486-46178-5

FIRST GERMAN READER: A Beginner's Dual-Language Book, Edited by Harry Steinhauer. Specially chosen for their power to evoke German life and culture, these short, simple readings include poems, stories, essays, and anecdotes by Goethe, Hesse, Heine, Schiller, and others. 224pp. 5⅜ x 8½. 0-486-46179-3

FIRST SPANISH READER: A Beginner's Dual-Language Book, Angel Flores. Delightful stories, other material based on works of Don Juan Manuel, Luis Taboada, Ricardo Palma, other noted writers. Complete faithful English translations on facing pages. Exercises. 176pp. 5⅜ x 8½. 0-486-25810-6

Browse over 9,000 books at www.doverpublications.com

FIVE ACRES AND INDEPENDENCE, Maurice G. Kains. Great back-to-the-land classic explains basics of self-sufficient farming. The one book to get. 95 illustrations. 397pp. 5⅜ x 8½. 0-486-20974-1

FLAGG'S SMALL HOUSES: Their Economic Design and Construction, 1922, Ernest Flagg. Although most famous for his skyscrapers, Flagg was also a proponent of the well-designed single-family dwelling. His classic treatise features innovations that save space, materials, and cost. 526 illustrations. 160pp. 9⅜ x 12¼. 0-486-45197-6

FLATLAND: A Romance of Many Dimensions, Edwin A. Abbott. Classic of science (and mathematical) fiction — charmingly illustrated by the author — describes the adventures of A. Square, a resident of Flatland, in Spaceland (three dimensions), Lineland (one dimension), and Pointland (no dimensions). 96pp. 5³⁄₁₆ x 8¼. 0-486-27263-X

FRANKENSTEIN, Mary Shelley. The story of Victor Frankenstein's monstrous creation and the havoc it caused has enthralled generations of readers and inspired countless writers of horror and suspense. With the author's own 1831 introduction. 176pp. 5³⁄₁₆ x 8¼. 0-486-28211-2

THE GARGOYLE BOOK: 572 Examples from Gothic Architecture, Lester Burbank Bridaham. Dispelling the conventional wisdom that French Gothic architectural flourishes were born of despair or gloom, Bridaham reveals the whimsical nature of these creations and the ingenious artisans who made them. 572 illustrations. 224pp. 8⅜ x 11. 0-486-44754-5

THE GIFT OF THE MAGI AND OTHER SHORT STORIES, O. Henry. Sixteen captivating stories by one of America's most popular storytellers. Included are such classics as "The Gift of the Magi," "The Last Leaf," and "The Ransom of Red Chief." Publisher's Note. 96pp. 5³⁄₁₆ x 8¼. 0-486-27061-0

THE GOETHE TREASURY: Selected Prose and Poetry, Johann Wolfgang von Goethe. Edited, Selected, and with an Introduction by Thomas Mann. In addition to his lyric poetry, Goethe wrote travel sketches, autobiographical studies, essays, letters, and proverbs in rhyme and prose. This collection presents outstanding examples from each genre. 368pp. 5⅜ x 8½. 0-486-44780-4

GREAT EXPECTATIONS, Charles Dickens. Orphaned Pip is apprenticed to the dirty work of the forge but dreams of becoming a gentleman — and one day finds himself in possession of "great expectations." Dickens' finest novel. 400pp. 5³⁄₁₆ x 8¼. 0-486-41586-4

GREAT WRITERS ON THE ART OF FICTION: From Mark Twain to Joyce Carol Oates, Edited by James Daley. An indispensable source of advice and inspiration, this anthology features essays by Henry James, Kate Chopin, Willa Cather, Sinclair Lewis, Jack London, Raymond Chandler, Raymond Carver, Eudora Welty, and Kurt Vonnegut, Jr. 192pp. 5⅜ x 8½. 0-486-45128-3

HAMLET, William Shakespeare. The quintessential Shakespearean tragedy, whose highly charged confrontations and anguished soliloquies probe depths of human feeling rarely sounded in any art. Reprinted from an authoritative British edition complete with illuminating footnotes. 128pp. 5³⁄₁₆ x 8¼. 0-486-27278-8

THE HAUNTED HOUSE, Charles Dickens. A Yuletide gathering in an eerie country retreat provides the backdrop for Dickens and his friends — including Elizabeth Gaskell and Wilkie Collins — who take turns spinning supernatural yarns. 144pp. 5⅜ x 8½. 0-486-46309-5

HEART OF DARKNESS, Joseph Conrad. Dark allegory of a journey up the Congo River and the narrator's encounter with the mysterious Mr. Kurtz. Masterly blend of adventure, character study, psychological penetration. For many, Conrad's finest, most enigmatic story. 80pp. 5³⁄₁₆ x 8¼. 0-486-26464-5

HENSON AT THE NORTH POLE, Matthew A. Henson. This thrilling memoir by the heroic African-American who was Peary's companion through two decades of Arctic exploration recounts a tale of danger, courage, and determination. "Fascinating and exciting." — *Commonweal.* 128pp. 5⅜ x 8½. 0-486-45472-X

HISTORIC COSTUMES AND HOW TO MAKE THEM, Mary Fernald and E. Shenton. Practical, informative guidebook shows how to create everything from short tunics worn by Saxon men in the fifth century to a lady's bustle dress of the late 1800s. 81 illustrations. 176pp. 5⅜ x 8½. 0-486-44906-8

THE HOUND OF THE BASKERVILLES, Arthur Conan Doyle. A deadly curse in the form of a legendary ferocious beast continues to claim its victims from the Baskerville family until Holmes and Watson intervene. Often called the best detective story ever written. 128pp. 5³⁄₁₆ x 8¼. 0-486-28214-7

THE HOUSE BEHIND THE CEDARS, Charles W. Chesnutt. Originally published in 1900, this groundbreaking novel by a distinguished African-American author recounts the drama of a brother and sister who "pass for white" during the dangerous days of Reconstruction. 208pp. 5⅜ x 8½. 0-486-46144-0

THE HUMAN FIGURE IN MOTION, Eadweard Muybridge. The 4,789 photographs in this definitive selection show the human figure — models almost all undraped — engaged in over 160 different types of action: running, climbing stairs, etc. 390pp. 7⅞ x 10⅝. 0-486-20204-6

THE IMPORTANCE OF BEING EARNEST, Oscar Wilde. Wilde's witty and buoyant comedy of manners, filled with some of literature's most famous epigrams, reprinted from an authoritative British edition. Considered Wilde's most perfect work. 64pp. 5³⁄₁₆ x 8¼. 0-486-26478-5

THE INFERNO, Dante Alighieri. Translated and with notes by Henry Wadsworth Longfellow. The first stop on Dante's famous journey from Hell to Purgatory to Paradise, this 14th-century allegorical poem blends vivid and shocking imagery with graceful lyricism. Translated by the beloved 19th-century poet, Henry Wadsworth Longfellow. 256pp. 5³⁄₁₆ x 8¼. 0-486-44288-8

JANE EYRE, Charlotte Brontë. Written in 1847, *Jane Eyre* tells the tale of an orphan girl's progress from the custody of cruel relatives to an oppressive boarding school and its culmination in a troubled career as a governess. 448pp. 5³⁄₁₆ x 8¼.
0-486-42449-9

JAPANESE WOODBLOCK FLOWER PRINTS, Tanigami Kônan. Extraordinary collection of Japanese woodblock prints by a well-known artist features 120 plates in brilliant color. Realistic images from a rare edition include daffodils, tulips, and other familiar and unusual flowers. 128pp. 11 x 8¼. 0-486-46442-3

JEWELRY MAKING AND DESIGN, Augustus F. Rose and Antonio Cirino. Professional secrets of jewelry making are revealed in a thorough, practical guide. Over 200 illustrations. 306pp. 5⅜ x 8½. 0-486-21750-7

JULIUS CAESAR, William Shakespeare. Great tragedy based on Plutarch's account of the lives of Brutus, Julius Caesar and Mark Antony. Evil plotting, ringing oratory, high tragedy with Shakespeare's incomparable insight, dramatic power. Explanatory footnotes. 96pp. 5³⁄₁₆ x 8¼. 0-486-26876-4

THE JUNGLE, Upton Sinclair. 1906 bestseller shockingly reveals intolerable labor practices and working conditions in the Chicago stockyards as it tells the grim story of a Slavic family that emigrates to America full of optimism but soon faces despair. 320pp. 5³⁄₁₆ x 8¼. 0-486-41923-1

THE KINGDOM OF GOD IS WITHIN YOU, Leo Tolstoy. The soul-searching book that inspired Gandhi to embrace the concept of passive resistance, Tolstoy's 1894 polemic clearly outlines a radical, well-reasoned revision of traditional Christian thinking. 352pp. 5³⁄₁₆ x 8¼. 0-486-45138-0

THE LADY OR THE TIGER?: and Other Logic Puzzles, Raymond M. Smullyan. Created by a renowned puzzle master, these whimsically themed challenges involve paradoxes about probability, time, and change; metapuzzles; and self-referentiality. Nineteen chapters advance in difficulty from relatively simple to highly complex. 1982 edition. 240pp. 5⅜ x 8½. 0-486-47027-X

LEAVES OF GRASS: The Original 1855 Edition, Walt Whitman. Whitman's immortal collection includes some of the greatest poems of modern times, including his masterpiece, "Song of Myself." Shattering standard conventions, it stands as an unabashed celebration of body and nature. 128pp. 5³⁄₁₆ x 8¼. 0-486-45676-5

LES MISÉRABLES, Victor Hugo. Translated by Charles E. Wilbour. Abridged by James K. Robinson. A convict's heroic struggle for justice and redemption plays out against a fiery backdrop of the Napoleonic wars. This edition features the excellent original translation and a sensitive abridgment. 304pp. 6⅛ x 9¼.
0-486-45789-3

LILITH: A Romance, George MacDonald. In this novel by the father of fantasy literature, a man travels through time to meet Adam and Eve and to explore humanity's fall from grace and ultimate redemption. 240pp. 5⅜ x 8½.
0-486-46818-6

THE LOST LANGUAGE OF SYMBOLISM, Harold Bayley. This remarkable book reveals the hidden meaning behind familiar images and words, from the origins of Santa Claus to the fleur-de-lys, drawing from mythology, folklore, religious texts, and fairy tales. 1,418 illustrations. 784pp. 5⅜ x 8½. 0-486-44787-1

MACBETH, William Shakespeare. A Scottish nobleman murders the king in order to succeed to the throne. Tortured by his conscience and fearful of discovery, he becomes tangled in a web of treachery and deceit that ultimately spells his doom. 96pp. 5³⁄₁₆ x 8¼. 0-486-27802-6

MAKING AUTHENTIC CRAFTSMAN FURNITURE: Instructions and Plans for 62 Projects, Gustav Stickley. Make authentic reproductions of handsome, functional, durable furniture: tables, chairs, wall cabinets, desks, a hall tree, and more. Construction plans with drawings, schematics, dimensions, and lumber specs reprinted from 1900s *The Craftsman* magazine. 128pp. 8⅛ x 11. 0-486-25000-8

MATHEMATICS FOR THE NONMATHEMATICIAN, Morris Kline. Erudite and entertaining overview follows development of mathematics from ancient Greeks to present. Topics include logic and mathematics, the fundamental concept, differential calculus, probability theory, much more. Exercises and problems. 641pp. 5⅜ x 8½. 0-486-24823-2

MEMOIRS OF AN ARABIAN PRINCESS FROM ZANZIBAR, Emily Ruete. This 19th-century autobiography offers a rare inside look at the society surrounding a sultan's palace. A real-life princess in exile recalls her vanished world of harems, slave trading, and court intrigues. 288pp. 5⅜ x 8½. 0-486-47121-7

THE METAMORPHOSIS AND OTHER STORIES, Franz Kafka. Excellent new English translations of title story (considered by many critics Kafka's most perfect work), plus "The Judgment," "In the Penal Colony," "A Country Doctor," and "A Report to an Academy." Note. 96pp. 5¾₆ x 8¼. 0-486-29030-1

MICROSCOPIC ART FORMS FROM THE PLANT WORLD, R. Anheisser. From undulating curves to complex geometrics, a world of fascinating images abound in this classic, illustrated survey of microscopic plants. Features 400 detailed illustrations of nature's minute but magnificent handiwork. The accompanying CD-ROM includes all of the images in the book. 128pp. 9 x 9. 0-486-46013-4

A MIDSUMMER NIGHT'S DREAM, William Shakespeare. Among the most popular of Shakespeare's comedies, this enchanting play humorously celebrates the vagaries of love as it focuses upon the intertwined romances of several pairs of lovers. Explanatory footnotes. 80pp. 5¾₆ x 8¼. 0-486-27067-X

THE MONEY CHANGERS, Upton Sinclair. Originally published in 1908, this cautionary novel from the author of *The Jungle* explores corruption within the American system as a group of power brokers joins forces for personal gain, triggering a crash on Wall Street. 192pp. 5⅜ x 8½. 0-486-46917-4

THE MOST POPULAR HOMES OF THE TWENTIES, William A. Radford. With a New Introduction by Daniel D. Reiff. Based on a rare 1925 catalog, this architectural showcase features floor plans, construction details, and photos of 26 homes, plus articles on entrances, porches, garages, and more. 250 illustrations, 21 color plates. 176pp. 8⅜ x 11. 0-486-47028-8

MY 66 YEARS IN THE BIG LEAGUES, Connie Mack. With a New Introduction by Rich Westcott. A Founding Father of modern baseball, Mack holds the record for most wins — and losses — by a major league manager. Enhanced by 70 photographs, his warmhearted autobiography is populated by many legends of the game. 288pp. 5⅜ x 8½. 0-486-47184-5

NARRATIVE OF THE LIFE OF FREDERICK DOUGLASS, Frederick Douglass. Douglass's graphic depictions of slavery, harrowing escape to freedom, and life as a newspaper editor, eloquent orator, and impassioned abolitionist. 96pp. 5¾₆ x 8¼. 0-486-28499-9

THE NIGHTLESS CITY: Geisha and Courtesan Life in Old Tokyo, J. E. de Becker. This unsurpassed study from 100 years ago ventured into Tokyo's red-light district to survey geisha and courtesan life and offer meticulous descriptions of training, dress, social hierarchy, and erotic practices. 49 black-and-white illustrations; 2 maps. 496pp. 5⅜ x 8½. 0-486-45563-7

THE ODYSSEY, Homer. Excellent prose translation of ancient epic recounts adventures of the homeward-bound Odysseus. Fantastic cast of gods, giants, cannibals, sirens, other supernatural creatures — true classic of Western literature. 256pp. 5¾₆ x 8¼. 0-486-40654-7

OEDIPUS REX, Sophocles. Landmark of Western drama concerns the catastrophe that ensues when King Oedipus discovers he has inadvertently killed his father and married his mother. Masterly construction, dramatic irony. Explanatory footnotes. 64pp. 5¾₆ x 8¼. 0-486-26877-2

ONCE UPON A TIME: The Way America Was, Eric Sloane. Nostalgic text and drawings brim with gentle philosophies and descriptions of how we used to live — self-sufficiently — on the land, in homes, and among the things built by hand. 44 line illustrations. 64pp. 8⅜ x 11. 0-486-44411-2